CUT AND CREATE!

MOTHER GOOSE

EASY STEP-BY-STEP PROJECTS THAT TEACH SCISSOR SKILLS

Written and illustrated by Kim Rankin

Teaching & Learning Company

1204 Buchanan St., P.O. Box 10

Carthage, IL 62321-0010

This book belongs to

SUE DROGOS

Cover by Kim Rankin

Copyright © 1998, Teaching & Learning Company

ISBN No. 1-57310-116-8

Printing No. 987654321

Teaching & Learning Company
1204 Buchanan St., P.O. Box 10
Carthage, IL 62321-0010

TABLE OF CONTENTS

PROJECTS

MOTHER GOOSE RHYMES

TLC10116 Copyright © Teaching & Learning Company, Carthage, IL 62321-0010

Dear Teacher or Parent,

"I did it myself" is a phrase which can be the foundation for a lifetime of accomplishment and positive self-esteem.

Cut and Create activities can be used by the teacher or parent to develop a variety of important early skills and to provide projects in which children can take pride and succeed.

- Simple patterns and easy, step-by-step directions develop scissor skills and give practice in visual-motor coordination. The scissor rating system in the upper right-hand corner on the first page of each project quickly identifies the easiest projects (✂), moderate (✂ ✂) and challenging (✂ ✂ ✂).
- Materials used are inexpensive and readily available.
- Finished products are fun, colorful and have myriad uses from play items to props; room decorations for walls, bulletin boards or mobiles; learning center manipulatives for counting, sorting, classifying or labeling; gifts or favors for parties or guests; and much more.

The simple and fun activities included in this book will help young learners build a solid base for a variety of skills such as: following directions, observation, discrimination and information processing. Various learning styles are addressed including visual, auditory and tactile.

Your art program, whether structured or serendipitous, can benefit from these simple and sequenced scissor skill activities. Your students will

- develop manual dexterity
- communicate
- learn to control his or her environment by being responsible for tools and materials
- observe
- discriminate (by color, shape, texture)
- sort, order, group and engage in other math processes
- imagine!

We hope you and your students will enjoy these projects. They have been designed to stimulate learning and creativity in a way that is simple and fun. So go cut and create! And have a good time!

Sincerely,

Kim

Kim Rankin

SUGGESTIONS FOR USING SOME OF THE PROJECTS

Different Uses

- Bulletin Boards
- Ceiling Decorations
- Flannel Board Figures
- Greeting Cards (Reduce 30-40%)
- Mobiles
- Paper Bag Puppets
- Party Favors
- Rebus Rhymes
- Refrigerator Magnets (Reduce 25-40%)
- Stick Puppets/Finger Puppets
- Tabletop or Desk Decorations
- Take-Homes for Parents
- Window/Door Decorations
- Portfolio Pieces
- Folders (Reduce 30-50%)

stick puppet

paper bag puppet

Bulletin Boards

Copy verse and related figures. Display on bulletin board covered with background paper. Add decorations (clouds, flowers, etc.) if you wish.

Little Bo Peep

Little Bo-Peep Has Lost Her Sheep

Little Bo-Peep has lost her sheep,
And can't tell where to find them;
Leave them alone, and they'll come home,
Bringing their tails behind them.

Rebus Rhymes

Copy the poem.
Use figures for words
wherever possible.

Hickory, dickory, dock;

The 🐭 ran up the 🕐;

The 🕐 struck 1,

And down he run,

Hickory, dickory, dock.

Mobiles

Here are two suggestions for making a mobile. One way is to use a sturdy paper plate for the top piece. Punch holes around the outer edge of the plate. Use string or yarn in random lengths to attach the ready-made patterns to the top piece.

Another way is to use sturdy tagboard. Cut a rectangle shape approximately 3" x 32" (8 x 56 cm) and staple the ends together to form a circle. Punch holes around the bottom edge. Use string or yarn in random lengths to attach the ready-made patterns. (Note: You will have to reduce the patterns 40 to 50% so they are not too big for the mobile.)

Greeting Cards

Celebrate a holiday or create an occasion. Handmade greeting cards are a surefire hit for parents, grandparents, relatives and friends. And what better way to say "thank you" to a visitor, custodian, principal, helper, etc.

Window/Door Decorations

Attach figures to door or window for a welcome-to-school, parent conference or special occasion display. Add extra pieces, if required. (Shown here: enlarged pumpkins [page 79].)

Flannel Board Figures

Cut figures from flannel instead of paper, or glue a piece of flannel or sandpaper to the back of the finished paper figure.

Little Bo-Peep

Little Bo-Peep has lost her sheep,
And can't tell where to find them;
Leave them alone, and they'll come
    home,
Bringing their tails behind them.

Mary Had a Little Lamb

Mary had a little lamb
    Its fleece was white as snow;
And everywhere that Mary went
    The lamb was sure to go.
It followed her to school one day,
    That was against the rule;
It made the children laugh and play,
    To see a lamb at school.

Little Boy Blue

Little boy blue,
    Come blow your horn;
The sheep's in the meadow;
    The cow's in the corn.
Where's the little boy
    That looks after the sheep?
He's under the haystack,
    Fast asleep.
Will you wake him?
    No, not I.
For if I do,
    He's sure to cry.

Baa, Baa, Black Sheep

Baa, baa, black sheep,
Have you any wool?
Yes, sir, yes, sir, three bags full:
One for the master, one for the dame
And one for the little boy that lives
    down the lane.

Materials: *black, dark gray and white paper; scissors; glue; black crayon or marker*
Optional Materials: *cotton balls or batting*

SHEEP/LAMB

1 Cut one #1 head from dark gray paper. Cut two #2 ears from black paper and glue to the back of the head as shown.

2 Cut one #3 body from white paper. Glue the head and ears to the body.

3 Cut one #4 forelock from white paper. Glue to the top of the head.

4 Cut one #5 tail from white paper and glue as shown. Cut two #6 eyes from white paper and glue on the head as illustrated.

5 Cut four #7 legs from black paper and glue as shown.

6 Cut four #8 hooves from black paper and glue to the bottoms of the legs as shown. Cut two #9 pupils from black paper and glue in place as shown. (Note: You could use a black crayon or marker to make the pupils.) Draw on a nose and mouth with black marker or crayon.

Note: Decorate the sheep's body and forelock with cotton balls or batting for fleece.

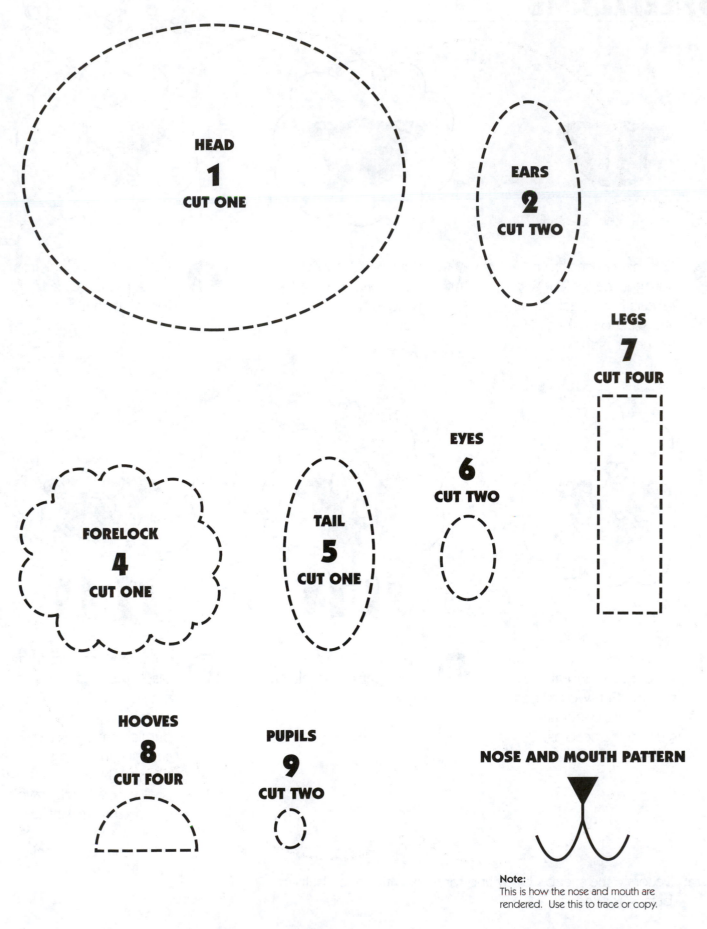

HEAD
1
CUT ONE

EARS
2
CUT TWO

LEGS
7
CUT FOUR

FORELOCK
4
CUT ONE

TAIL
5
CUT ONE

EYES
6
CUT TWO

HOOVES
8
CUT FOUR

PUPILS
9
CUT TWO

NOSE AND MOUTH PATTERN

Note:
This is how the nose and mouth are
rendered. Use this to trace or copy.

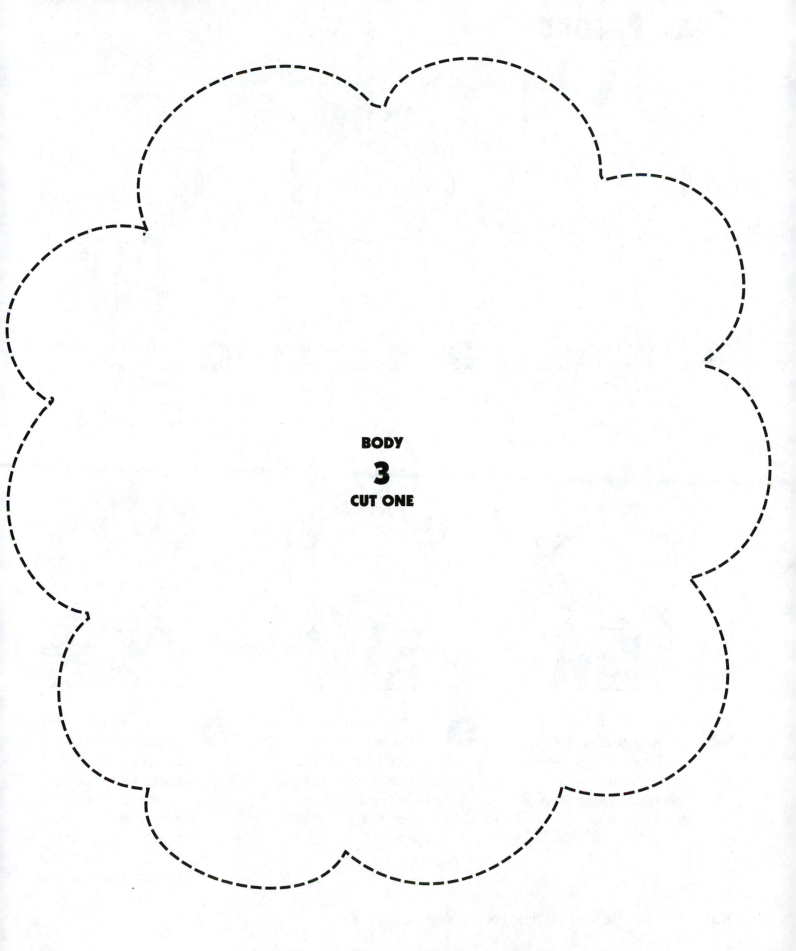

BODY

3

CUT ONE

Materials: *black, blue, brown, flesh-colored, a variety of colors and white paper; scissors; glue; black crayon or marker*

GIRL FIGURE

1 Cut one #1 head and two #2 ears from flesh-colored paper. Glue the ears to the back of the head as shown.

2 Cut one #3 hat from blue paper. Glue the head-piece on the hat as illustrated.

3 Cut one #4 body from your choice of paper. Glue the head and hat piece on top of the body as shown.

4 Cut two #5 hair from brown paper and glue as shown. Cut two #6 collars from your choice of paper. Glue to top of the body form.

5 Cut two #7 bows on top of the hair from your choice of paper and glue as shown. Cut one #8 button from black paper and glue to the collar.

6 Cut two #9 eyes from white paper. Cut two #10 pupils from black paper or use a black crayon or marker to draw the pupils. Draw on a mouth and a nose. Trace and cut out your handprints and glue as shown.

Note: You can use the facial features on page 74.

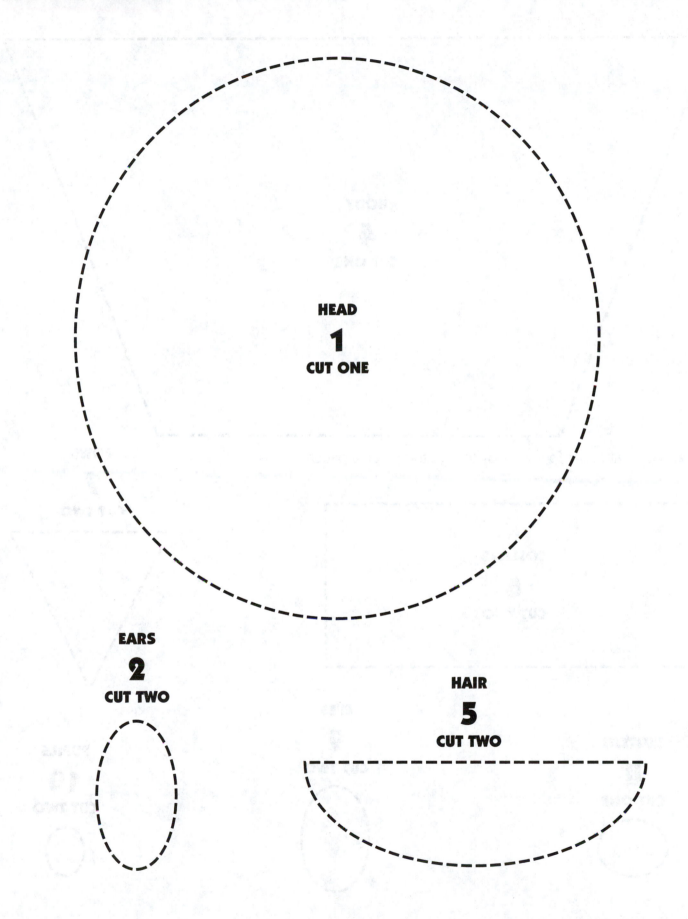

HEAD

1

CUT ONE

EARS

2

CUT TWO

HAIR

5

CUT TWO

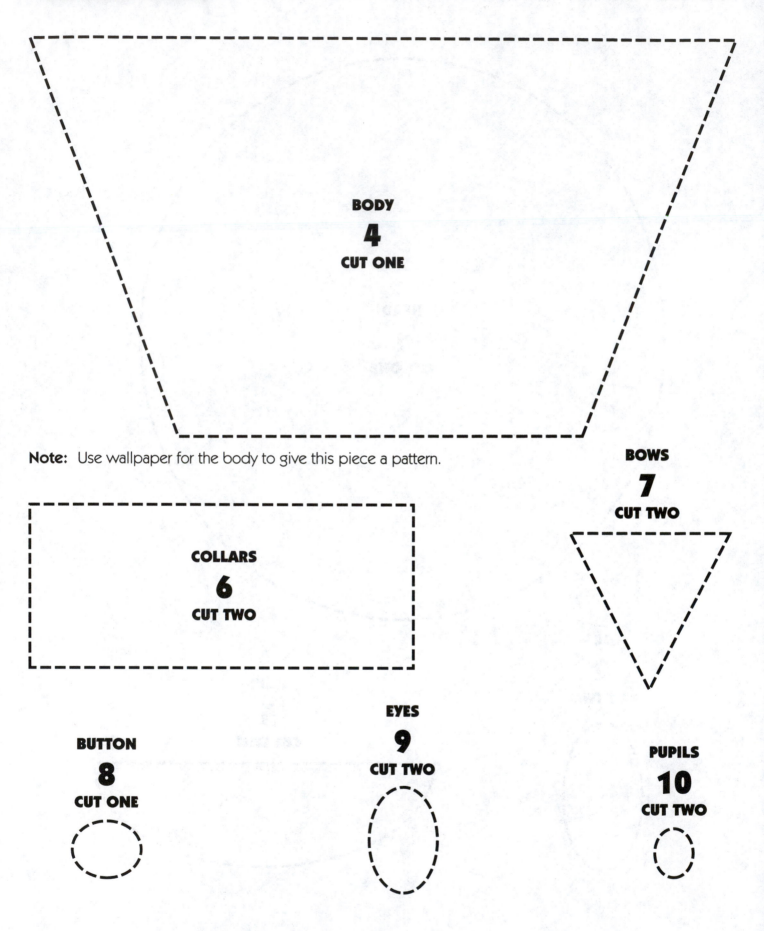

BODY
4
CUT ONE

Note: Use wallpaper for the body to give this piece a pattern.

COLLARS
6
CUT TWO

BOWS
7
CUT TWO

BUTTON
8
CUT ONE

EYES
9
CUT TWO

PUPILS
10
CUT TWO

GIRL FIGURE PATTERNS

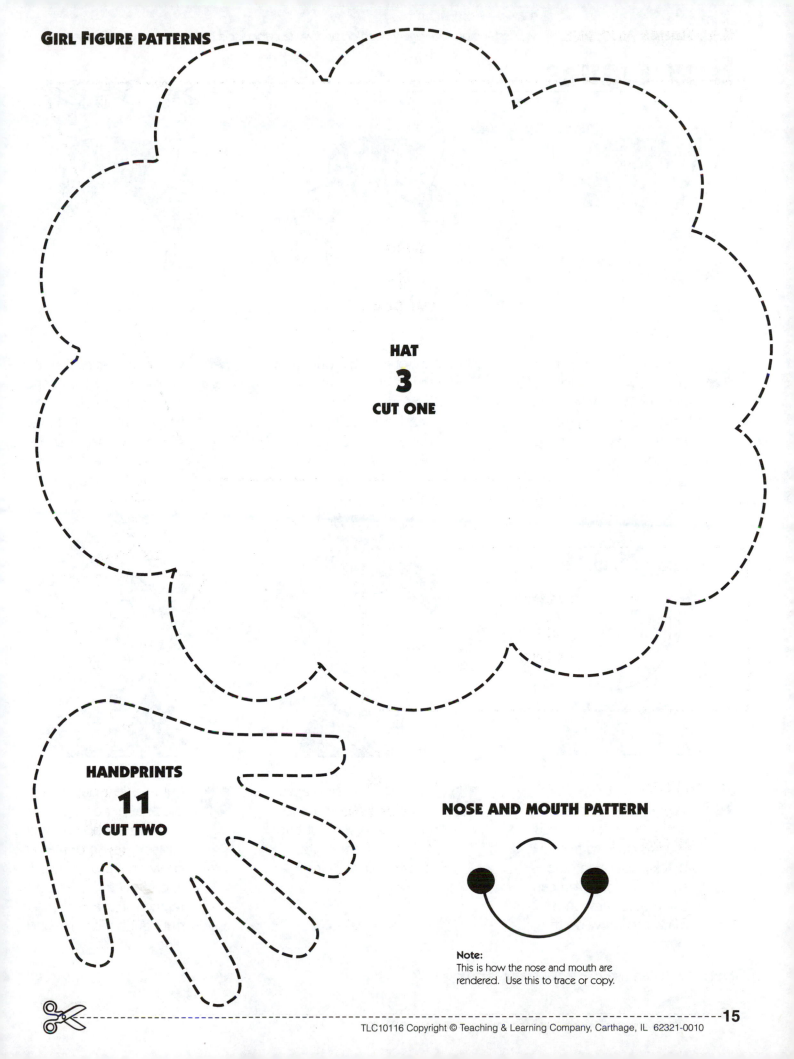

HAT
3
CUT ONE

HANDPRINTS
11
CUT TWO

NOSE AND MOUTH PATTERN

Note:
This is how the nose and mouth are
rendered. Use this to trace or copy.

Materials: black, blue, brown, flesh-colored, a variety of colors and white paper; scissors; glue; black crayon or marker

BOY FIGURE

1 Cut one #1 hat top from your choice of paper. Cut one #2 feather from yellow or white paper and glue on the hat top as shown.

2 Cut one #3 hat brim from the same color as your hat top. Cut one #4 head from flesh-colored paper and glue to the hat brim.

3 Cut two #5 ears from the flesh-colored paper and glue to the back of the head. Cut two #6 collars from white paper and glue to the back of the head as illustrated.

4 Cut one #7 body from your choice of paper and glue as shown. Cut four #8 buttons from black paper and glue as shown. (Note: You can use a black crayon or marker to draw on the buttons.)

5 Cut three #9 hair pieces from brown paper and glue as shown. Cut two #10 eyes from white paper and glue in place.

6 Cut two #11 pupils from black paper and glue on the eyes as shown. With a black crayon or marker, draw on a mouth, nose and the line in the feather. Trace and cut out your handprints and glue as shown.

Note: You can use the facial features on page 74.

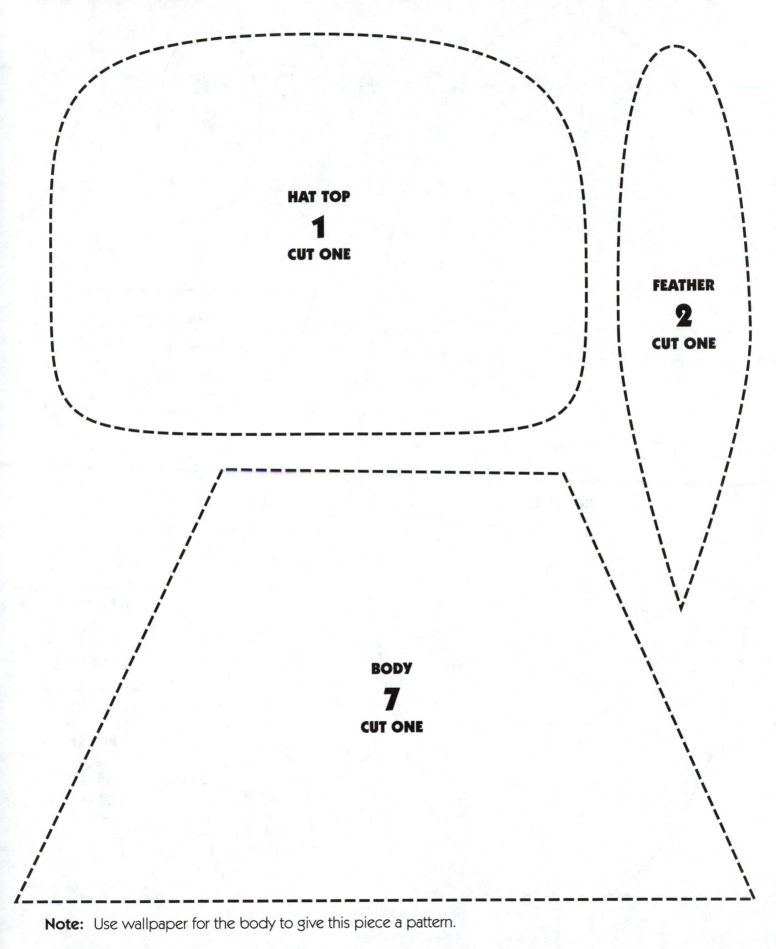

HAT TOP

1

CUT ONE

FEATHER

2

CUT ONE

BODY

7

CUT ONE

Note: Use wallpaper for the body to give this piece a pattern.

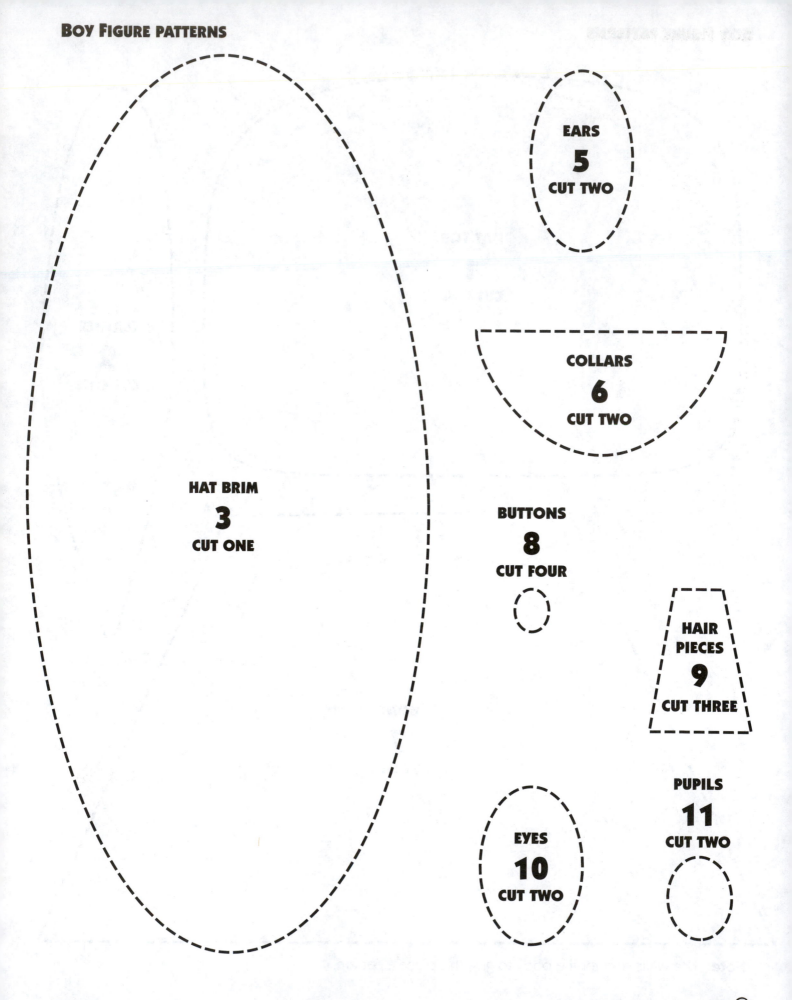

EARS
5
CUT TWO

COLLARS
6
CUT TWO

HAT BRIM
3
CUT ONE

BUTTONS
8
CUT FOUR

HAIR PIECES
9
CUT THREE

PUPILS
11
CUT TWO

EYES
10
CUT TWO

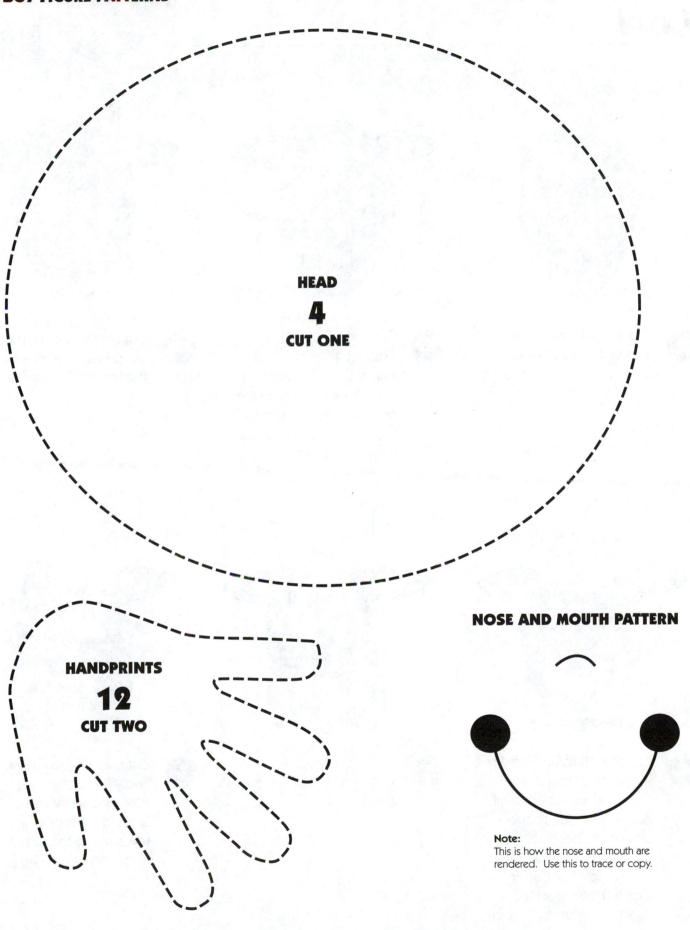

HEAD
4
CUT ONE

HANDPRINTS
12
CUT TWO

NOSE AND MOUTH PATTERN

Note:
This is how the nose and mouth are rendered. Use this to trace or copy.

Materials: *black, brown, red, tan and white paper; scissors; glue; black crayon or marker*

Cow

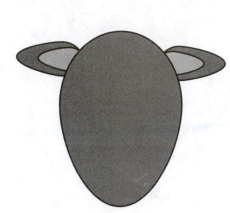

 1 Cut one #1 head from brown or red paper.

2 Cut two #2 inner ears from a lighter color of paper than the head. Cut two #3 ears from the same color of paper as the head and glue to the back of the ear pieces.

3 Cut two #4 horns from tan paper and glue to the top of the head as shown.

 4 Cut one #5 forelock from the same color chosen for the inner ear color of paper and glue to the top of the head as shown. Cut one #6 nose from a color of paper that is lighter than the head and glue as shown.

5 Cut two #7 eyes from white paper and glue in place.

6 Cut two #8 pupils and two #9 nostrils from black paper or use a black marker or crayon to draw on the pupils and nostrils.

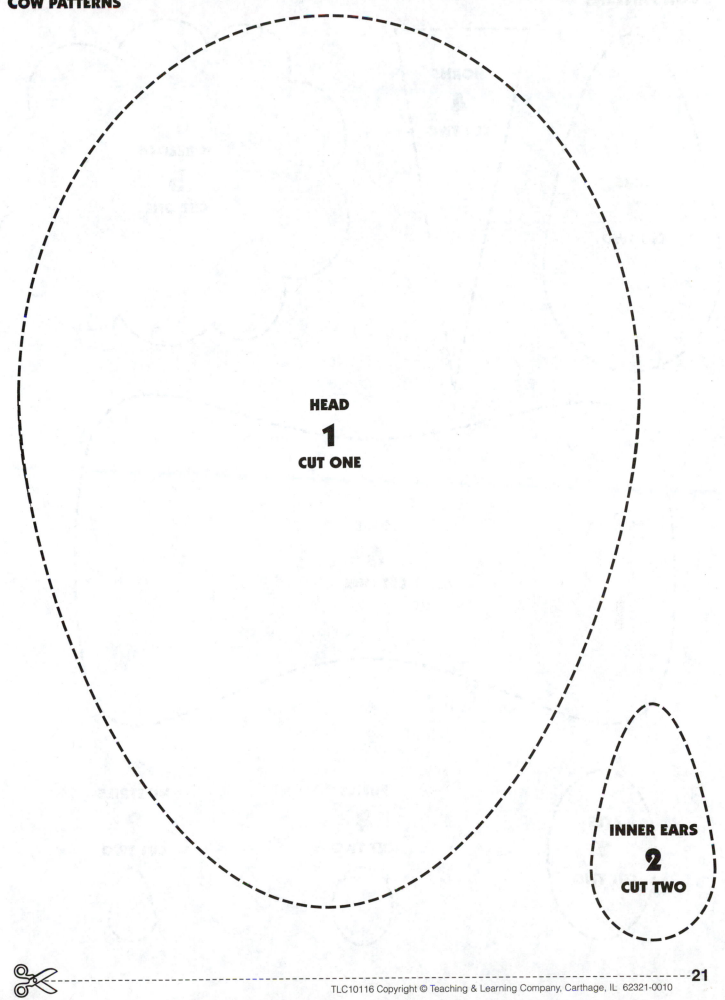

HEAD

1

CUT ONE

INNER EARS

2

CUT TWO

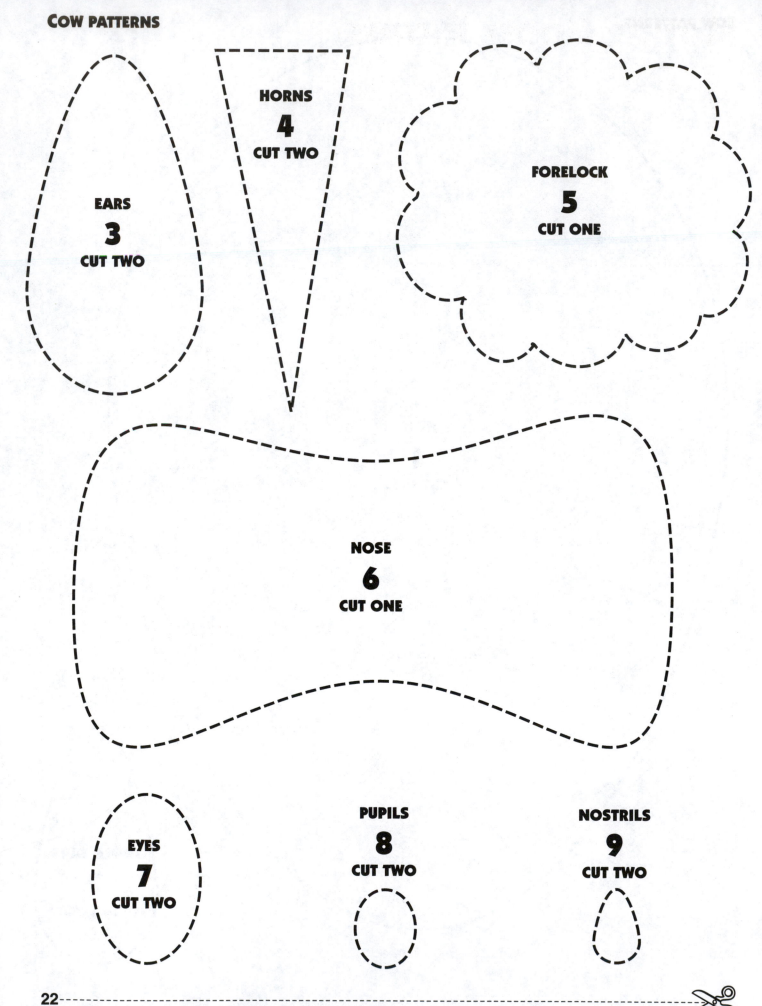

EARS
3
CUT TWO

HORNS
4
CUT TWO

FORELOCK
5
CUT ONE

NOSE
6
CUT ONE

EYES
7
CUT TWO

PUPILS
8
CUT TWO

NOSTRILS
9
CUT TWO

This Little Pig

This little pig went to market.
This little pig stayed at home.
This little pig had roast beef.
This little pig had none.
This little pig said, "Wee, wee, wee!"
All the way home.

Tom, Tom, the Piper's Son

Tom, Tom, the piper's son,
Stole a pig and away he run.
The pig was eat and Tom was beat,
And Tom went crying down the street.

Tom, Tom, the piper's son,
He learned to play when he was young,
But all the tunes that he could play
Were "Over the hills and far away."

To Market, to Market

To market, to market to buy a fat pig,
Home again, home again, jiggety-jig;
To market, to market to buy a fat hog,
Home again, home again, jiggety-jog.

Note: Use the project on page 16 to represent Tom, the piper's son.

LITTLE PIG 1

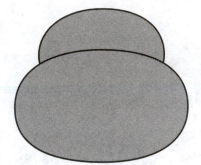
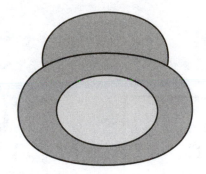

1 Cut one #1 head from pink paper. Cut one #2 face from pink paper and glue to the head as shown.

2 Cut one #3 snout from light pink paper and glue on the face as shown.

3 Cut one #4 ear and one #5 ear from pink paper and glue in place as shown.

4 Cut two #6 eyes from white paper and glue on the head as shown. Draw on the mouth and tongue with a black crayon or marker.

5 Cut two #7 nostrils from dark pink paper and glue on the snout as shown. Cut two #8 pupils from black paper and glue on the eyes as shown, or use a black crayon or marker to draw on the pupils.

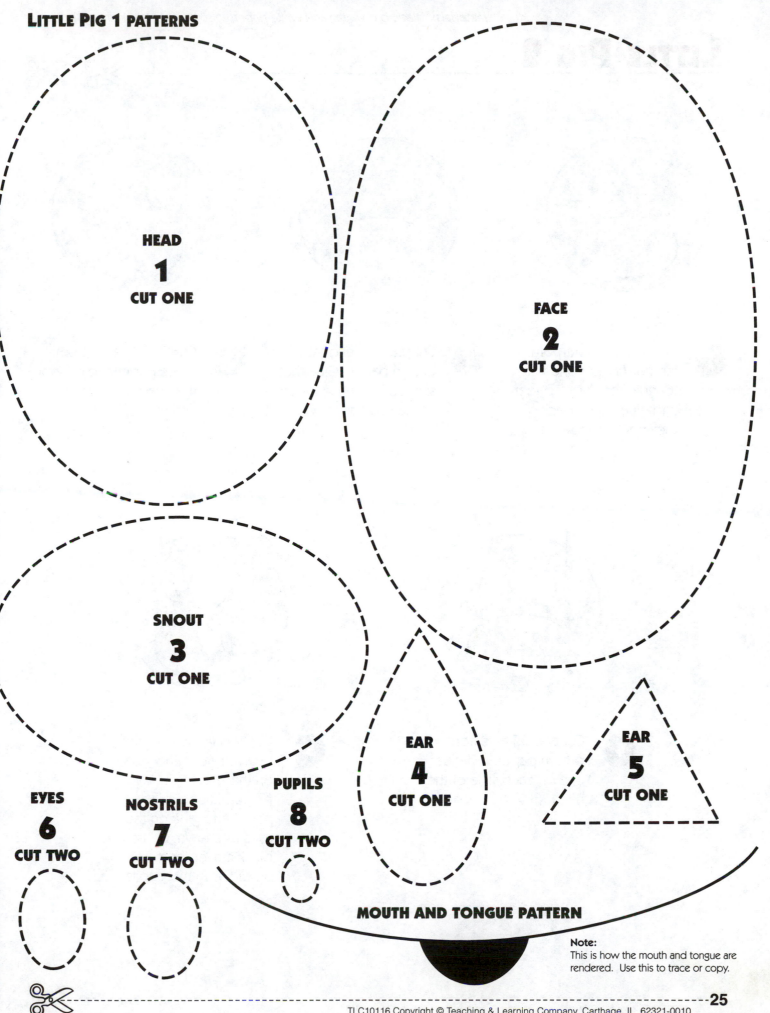

LITTLE PIG 1 PATTERNS

HEAD
1
CUT ONE

FACE
2
CUT ONE

SNOUT
3
CUT ONE

EYES
6
CUT TWO

NOSTRILS
7
CUT TWO

PUPILS
8
CUT TWO

EAR
4
CUT ONE

EAR
5
CUT ONE

MOUTH AND TONGUE PATTERN

Note:
This is how the mouth and tongue are rendered. Use this to trace or copy.

LITTLE PIG 2

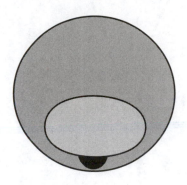

1 Cut one #1 snout from tan paper. Cut one #2 tongue from black paper and glue to the back of the snout as shown.

2 Cut one #3 head from brown paper. Glue the snout and tongue piece to the head as shown.

3 Cut two #4 eyes from white paper and glue on the head place as shown.

4 Cut two #5 ears from brown paper and glue one on each side of the head.

5 Cut two #6 nostrils from brown paper and glue on the snout. Cut two #7 pupils from black paper and glue on the eyes as shown, or use a black crayon or marker on draw on the pupils.

LITTLE PIG 2 PATTERNS

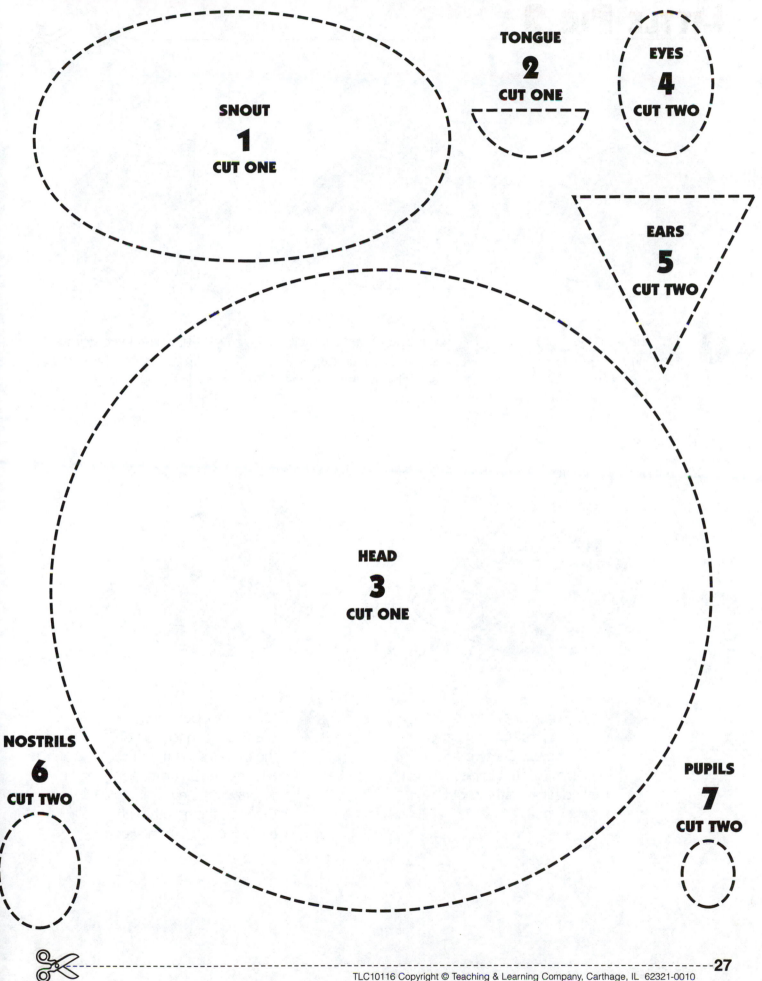

SNOUT
1
CUT ONE

TONGUE
2
CUT ONE

EYES
4
CUT TWO

EARS
5
CUT TWO

HEAD
3
CUT ONE

NOSTRILS
6
CUT TWO

PUPILS
7
CUT TWO

LITTLE PIG 3

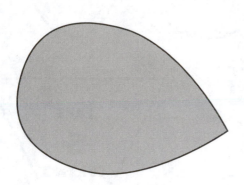

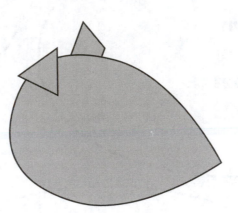

1 Cut one #1 head from tan paper.

2 Cut one #2 ear and one #3 ear from tan paper and glue to the head as shown.

3 Cut one #4 snout from lighter tan paper and glue as shown.

4 Cut one #5 eye from white paper and glue to the head. Cut two #6 nostrils from tan paper and glue on the snout as shown.

5 Cut one #7 pupil from black paper and glue on the eye as shown, or use a black crayon or marker to draw on the pupil. Draw on the mouth with a black crayon or marker.

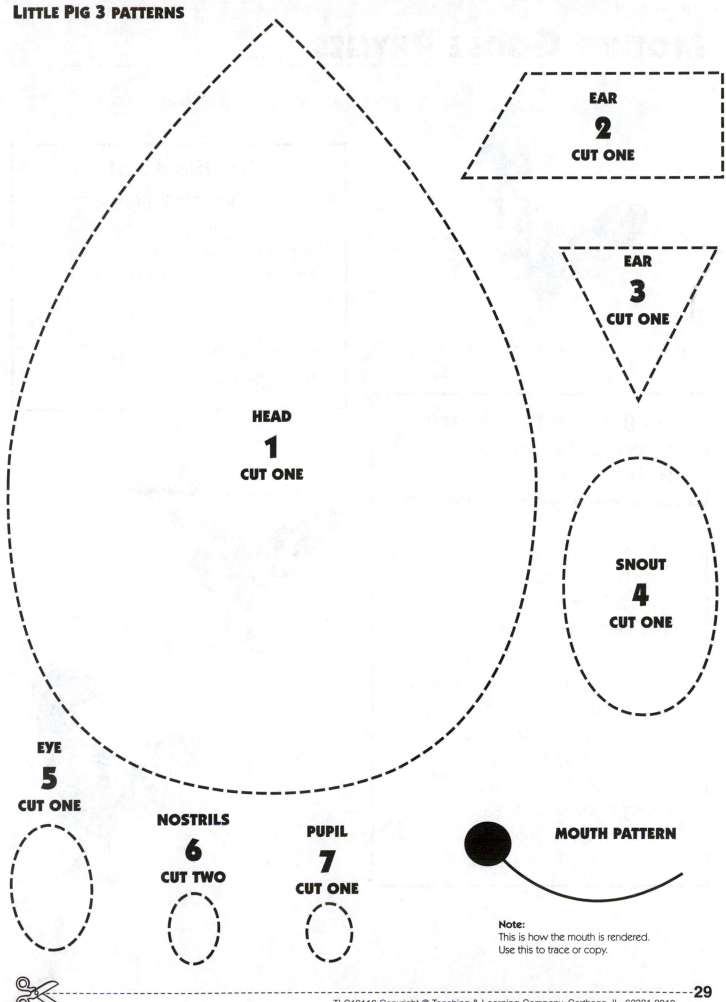

LITTLE PIG 3 PATTERNS

EAR
2
CUT ONE

EAR
3
CUT ONE

HEAD
1
CUT ONE

SNOUT
4
CUT ONE

EYE
5
CUT ONE

NOSTRILS
6
CUT TWO

PUPIL
7
CUT ONE

MOUTH PATTERN

Note:
This is how the mouth is rendered.
Use this to trace or copy.

Two Blackbirds

There were two blackbirds
Sitting on a hill.
The one named Jack,
And the other named Jill.
Fly away, Jack!
Fly away, Jill!
Come again, Jack!
Come again, Jill!

Sing a Song of Sixpence

Sing a song of sixpence,
A pocketful of rye;
Four-and-twenty blackbirds
Baked in a pie.
When the pie was opened,
The birds began to sing;
Wasn't that a dainty dish
To set before the king?

The king was in the countinghouse,
Counting out his money;
The queen was in the parlor,
Eating bread and honey.
The maid was in the garden,
Hanging out the clothes;
When down came a blackbird
And snipped off her nose.

BLACKBIRD JACK

1 Cut one #1 body from black paper. Cut one #2 tail feather from black paper. Glue the tail feather to the body as shown.

2 Cut one #3 tail feather from black paper and glue as shown.

3 Cut one #4 wing from black paper and glue to the body as illustrated.

4 Cut one #5 head from black paper and glue to the top of the body as shown.

5 Cut two #6 legs from gray paper and glue to the bottom of the body. Cut two #7 feet from gray paper and glue to the bottoms of the legs as shown.

6 Cut one #8 beak from gray paper and glue on the head. Cut one #9 eye from yellow paper, and cut one #10 pupil from black paper and glue on the head as shown.

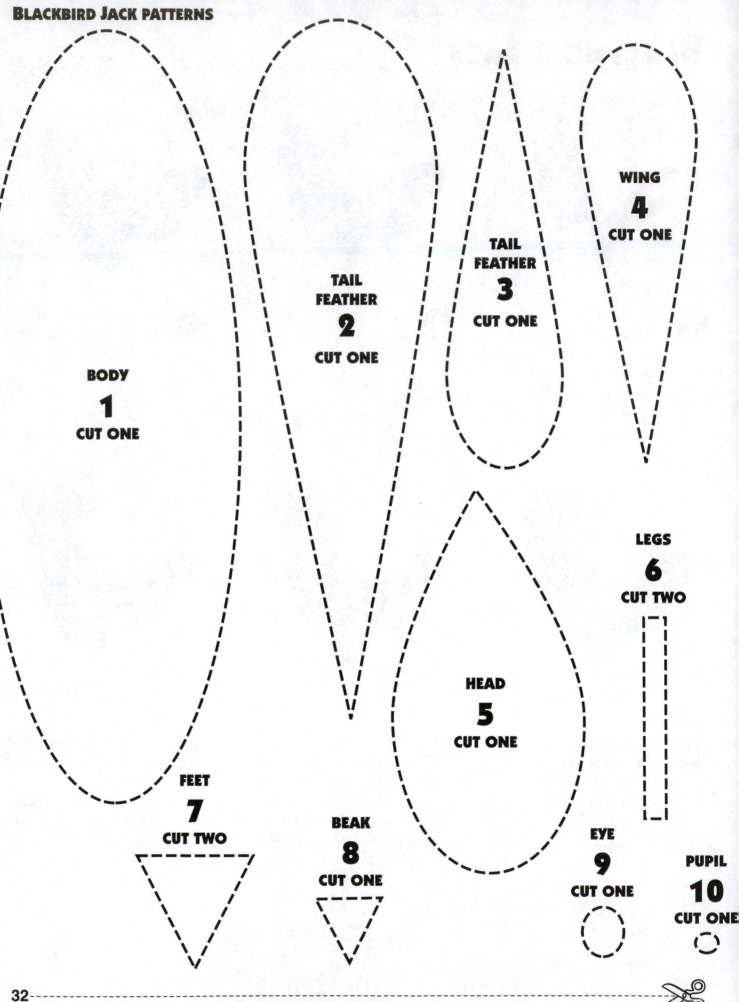

Materials: *black, gray and yellow paper; scissors; glue; black crayon or marker*

BLACKBIRD JILL

1 Cut one #1 body from black paper. Cut one #2 tail feather from black paper. Glue the tail feather to the body as shown.

2 Cut one #3 tail feather from black paper and glue as shown.

3 Cut one #4 head from black paper and glue to the top of the body as shown.

 4 Cut one #5 wing from black paper and glue to the body as illustrated.

5 Cut two #6 legs from gray paper and glue to the bottom of the body. Cut two #7 feet from gray paper and glue to the bottoms of the legs as shown.

6 Cut one #8 beak from gray paper and glue on the head. Cut one #9 eye from yellow paper, and cut one #10 pupil from black paper and glue on the head as shown.

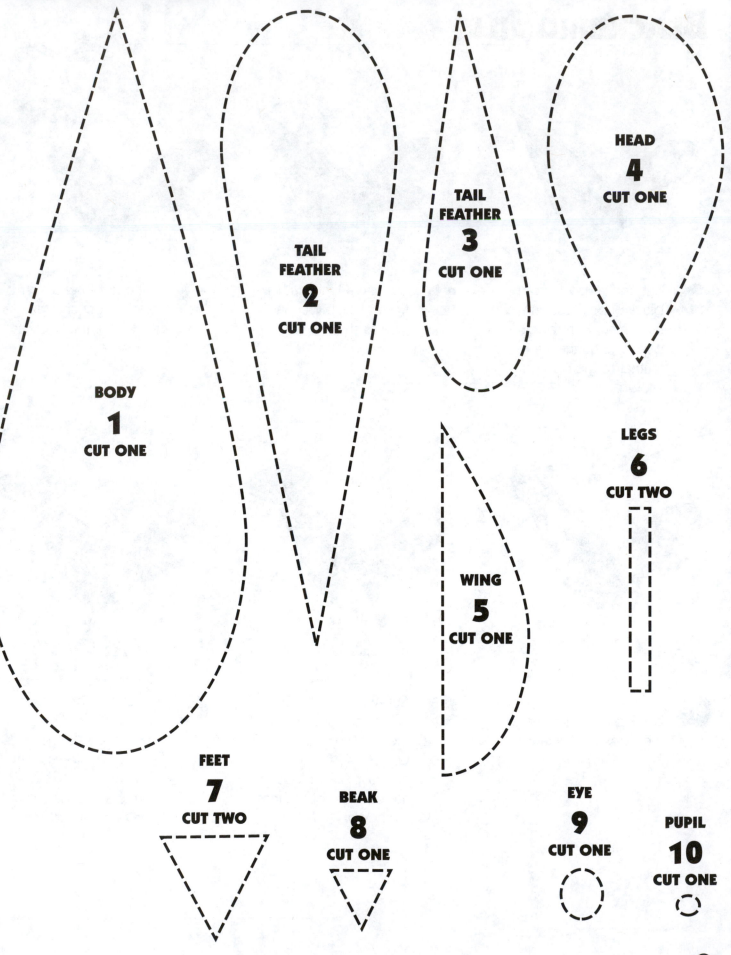

BODY
1
CUT ONE

TAIL
FEATHER
2
CUT ONE

TAIL
FEATHER
3
CUT ONE

HEAD
4
CUT ONE

LEGS
6
CUT TWO

WING
5
CUT ONE

FEET
7
CUT TWO

BEAK
8
CUT ONE

EYE
9
CUT ONE

PUPIL
10
CUT ONE

Three Little Kittens

Three little kittens they lost their
    mittens,
And they began to cry,
"Oh! Mammy dear,
We sadly fear,
Our mittens we have lost!"

"What! Lost your mittens,
You naughty kittens,
Then you shall have no pie."

Miew, miew, miew, miew,
Miew, miew, miew, miew.

The three little kittens they found
    their mittens,
And they began to cry.

"Oh! Mammy dear,
See here, see here,
Our mittens we have found."

"What! Found your mittens,
You darling kittens,
Then you shall have some pie."

Purr, purr, purr, purr,
Purr, purr, purr, purr.

I Love Little Pussy

I love little pussy, her coat is so
    warm,
And if I don't hurt her, she'll do me
    no harm.
So I'll not pull her tail, nor drive her
    away,
But pussy and I very gently will
    play.
I'll sit by the fire and give her some
    food,
And pussy will love me because I am
    good.

The Cat and the Fiddle

Hey, diddle, diddle,
The cat and the fiddle,
The cow jumped over the moon;
The little dog laughed to see such
    sport,
And the dish ran away with the
    spoon.

MOTHER GOOSE RHYMES

A Cat Came Fiddling

A cat came fiddling out of a barn,
With a pair of bagpipes under her
    arm;
She could sing nothing but fiddle-
    dee-dee,
The mouse has married the bumble-
    bee;
Pipe, cat; dance, mouse—
We'll have a wedding at our good
    house.

Hickory, Dickory, Dock

Hickory, dickory,
    dock;
The mouse ran up
    the clock;
The clock struck one,
And down he run,
Hickory, dickory,
    dock.

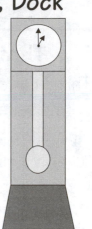

Ding, Dong Bell!

Ding, dong bell!
Pussy's in the well!
Who put her in?
Little Johnny Green.
Who pulled her out?
Little Johnny Stout.

What a naughty boy was that,
To try to drown poor pussy cat,
Which never did him any harm,
But killed the mice in his father's
    barn!

Pussy Cat, Pussy Cat

Pussy cat, pussy cat,
    Where have you been?
I've been to London
    To look at the Queen.
Pussy cat, pussy cat,
    What did you do there?
I frightened a little mouse
    Under her chair.

KITTEN

1 Cut one #1 head from your choice of paper. Cut two #2 ears from the same color paper as the head.

2 Cut two #3 inner ears from pink paper and glue to the #2 ears and then glue the ear pieces to the back of the head as shown.

3 Cut one #4 body from the same color you chose for the cat. Glue the head to the body as shown.

4 Cut one #5 back leg from the same color you chose for the cat and glue to the body as shown.

5 Cut three #6 feet from the same color of paper you chose for the cat. Glue two in place for the front feet as shown. Glue the other to the back leg. Cut one #7 tail from the same color of paper you chose for the cat and glue to the body as shown.

6 Cut two #8 eyes from white paper and glue on the head. Cut two #9 pupils from green paper and glue on the eyes as shown. Or use a marker to draw on the eyes. Use a black crayon or marker to draw slits in the middle of the pupils. Draw on the nose, mouth and claws as shown.

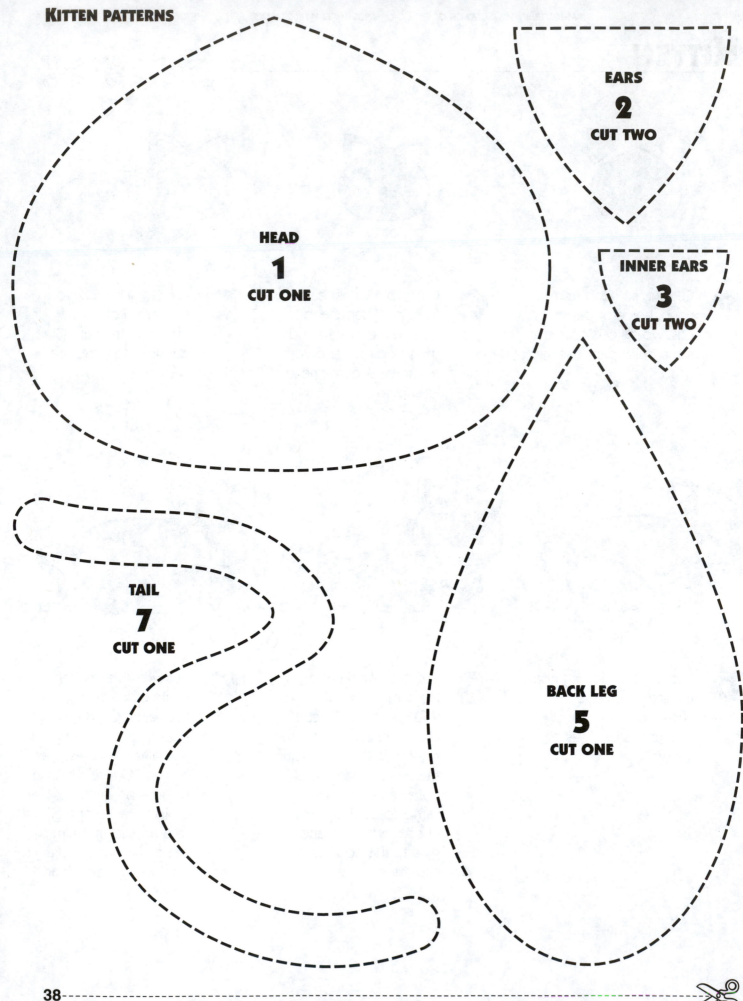

EARS
2
CUT TWO

HEAD
1
CUT ONE

INNER EARS
3
CUT TWO

TAIL
7
CUT ONE

BACK LEG
5
CUT ONE

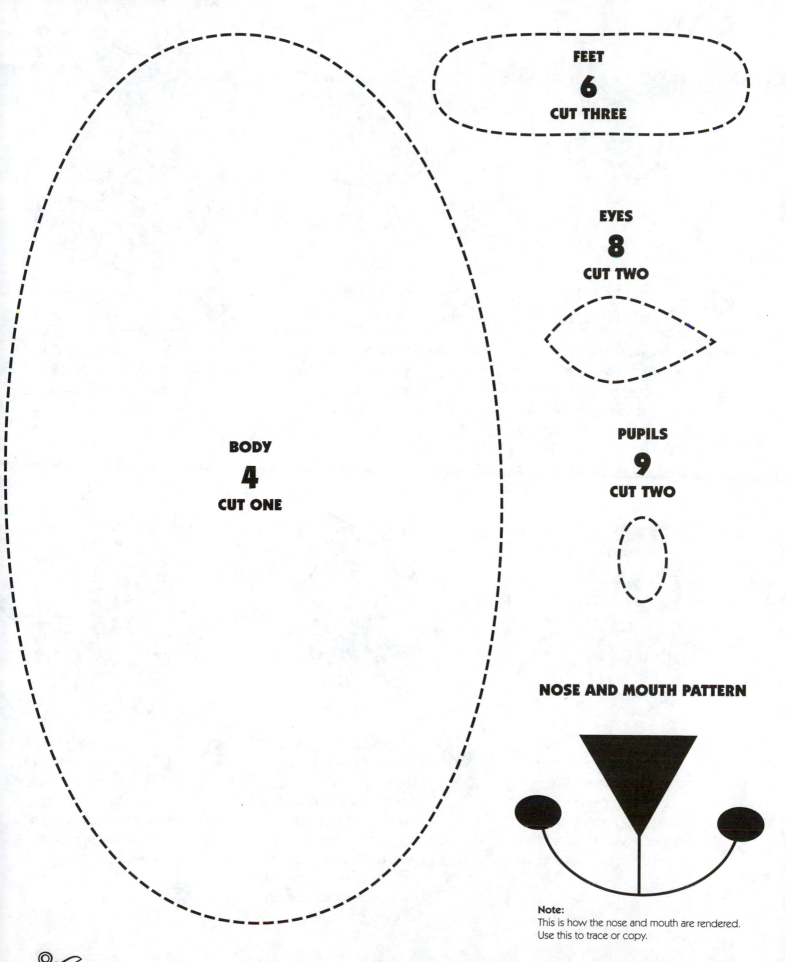

FEET
6
CUT THREE

EYES
8
CUT TWO

PUPILS
9
CUT TWO

BODY
4
CUT ONE

NOSE AND MOUTH PATTERN

Note:
This is how the nose and mouth are rendered.
Use this to trace or copy.

CAT

 Cut one #1 head from orange paper. Cut one #2 face from orange paper and glue to the head as shown. Cut two #3 ears from orange paper and two #4 inner ears from white paper. Glue the #4 ears on top of the #3 ears. Then glue the ear pieces to the back of the head as shown.

 Cut one #5 neck from orange paper and glue to the back of the head. Cut one #6 body from orange paper and glue to the bottom of the neck.

3 Cut two #7 legs from orange paper and glue one to each side of the back of the body. Cut one #8 tail from orange paper and glue in place as shown.

 Cut two #9 paws from orange paper and glue as shown. Cut two #10 eyes from white paper and two #11 eyelids from orange paper. Glue the eyelids on top of the eyes as shown.

5 Cut two #13 front paws from orange paper and glue as shown. Cut two #14 and six #15 paw prints from black paper and glue on the front paws as shown. Cut two #16 pupils from black paper and glue on the eyes as shown.

6 Cut one #17 nose from black paper and glue on the face as shown. With a black crayon or marker, draw on the claws, leg lines, whiskers, mouth and tongue.

CAT PATTERNS

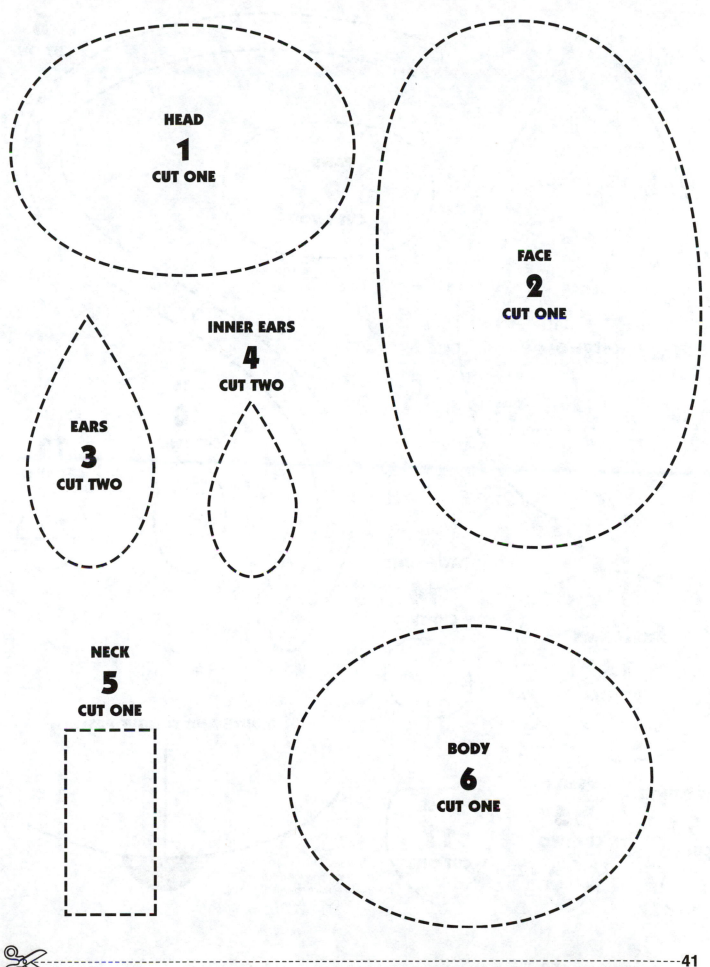

HEAD
1
CUT ONE

FACE
2
CUT ONE

INNER EARS
4
CUT TWO

EARS
3
CUT TWO

NECK
5
CUT ONE

BODY
6
CUT ONE

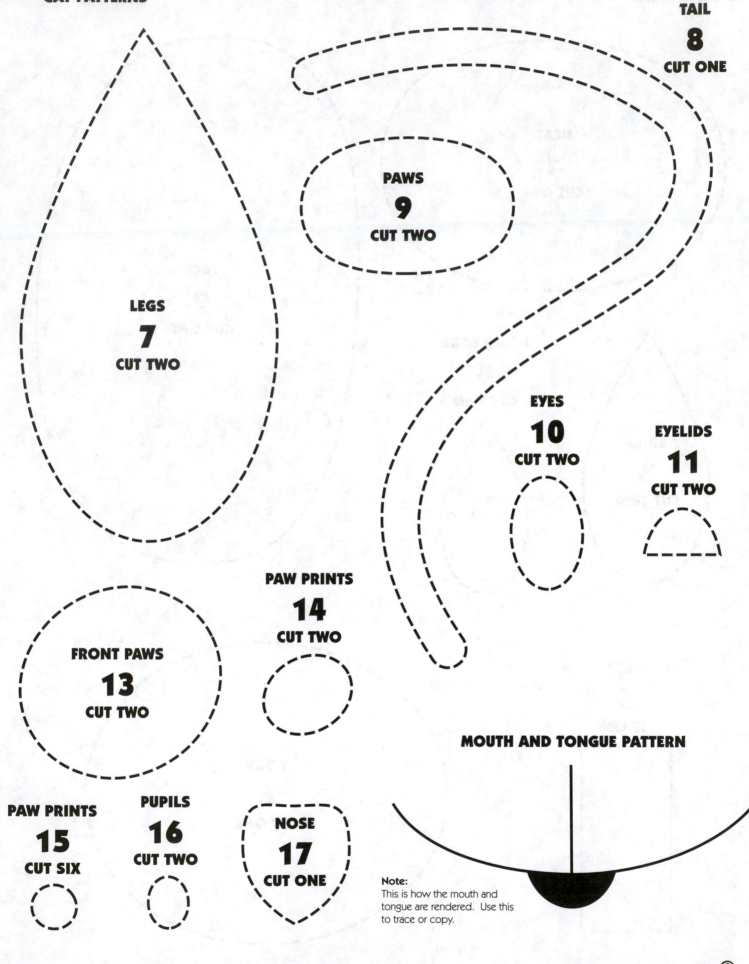

TAIL
8
CUT ONE

PAWS
9
CUT TWO

LEGS
7
CUT TWO

EYES
10
CUT TWO

EYELIDS
11
CUT TWO

PAW PRINTS
14
CUT TWO

FRONT PAWS
13
CUT TWO

MOUTH AND TONGUE PATTERN

PAW PRINTS
15
CUT SIX

PUPILS
16
CUT TWO

NOSE
17
CUT ONE

Note:
This is how the mouth and tongue are rendered. Use this to trace or copy.

COW

1 Cut one #1 head and one #2 nose from brown paper. Cut two #3 ears from brown paper. Cut two #4 inner ears from tan paper. Glue the #4 inner ears on top of the #3 ears. Glue the ear pieces to the back of the head as shown.

2 Cut two #5 horns from tan paper and glue to the head as shown.

3 Cut one #6 body from brown paper. Glue the headpiece to the body as shown. Cut two #7 spots from black paper and glue one to each side of the body as illustrated. Cut one #8 forelock from black paper and glue on the top of the head as shown.

4 Cut four #9 legs from brown paper and glue in place. Cut four #10 hooves from black paper and glue to the bottoms of the legs as shown.

5 Cut one #11 tail from black paper and one #12 tail from brown paper and glue as shown. Cut one #13 tongue from red paper and one #14 mouth from brown paper and glue the red tongue on top of the brown mouth. Then glue to the head of the cow as shown.

6 Cut two #15 eyes from white paper. Cut two #16 pupils from black paper and glue on the eyes. Then glue the eyes to the head as shown. Cut two #17 nostrils from brown paper and two #18 nostrils from black paper. Use a black crayon or marker to draw on the smile. Glue the #18 nostrils on top of the #17 nostrils. Glue the nostril pieces on the head as shown.

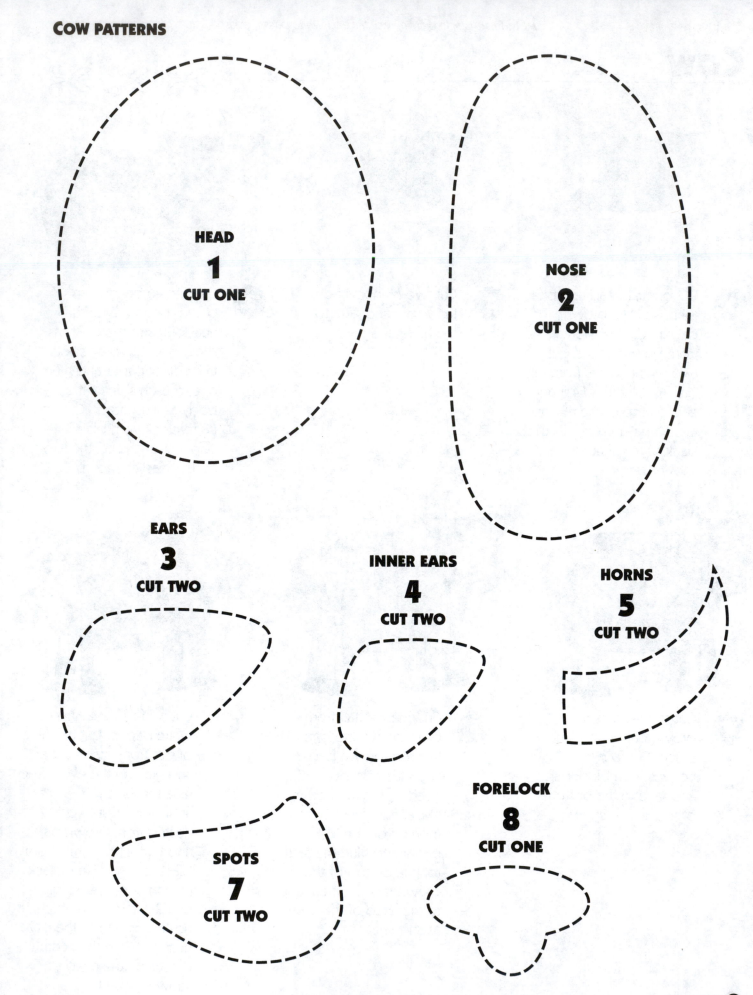

HEAD
1
CUT ONE

NOSE
2
CUT ONE

EARS
3
CUT TWO

INNER EARS
4
CUT TWO

HORNS
5
CUT TWO

FORELOCK
8
CUT ONE

SPOTS
7
CUT TWO

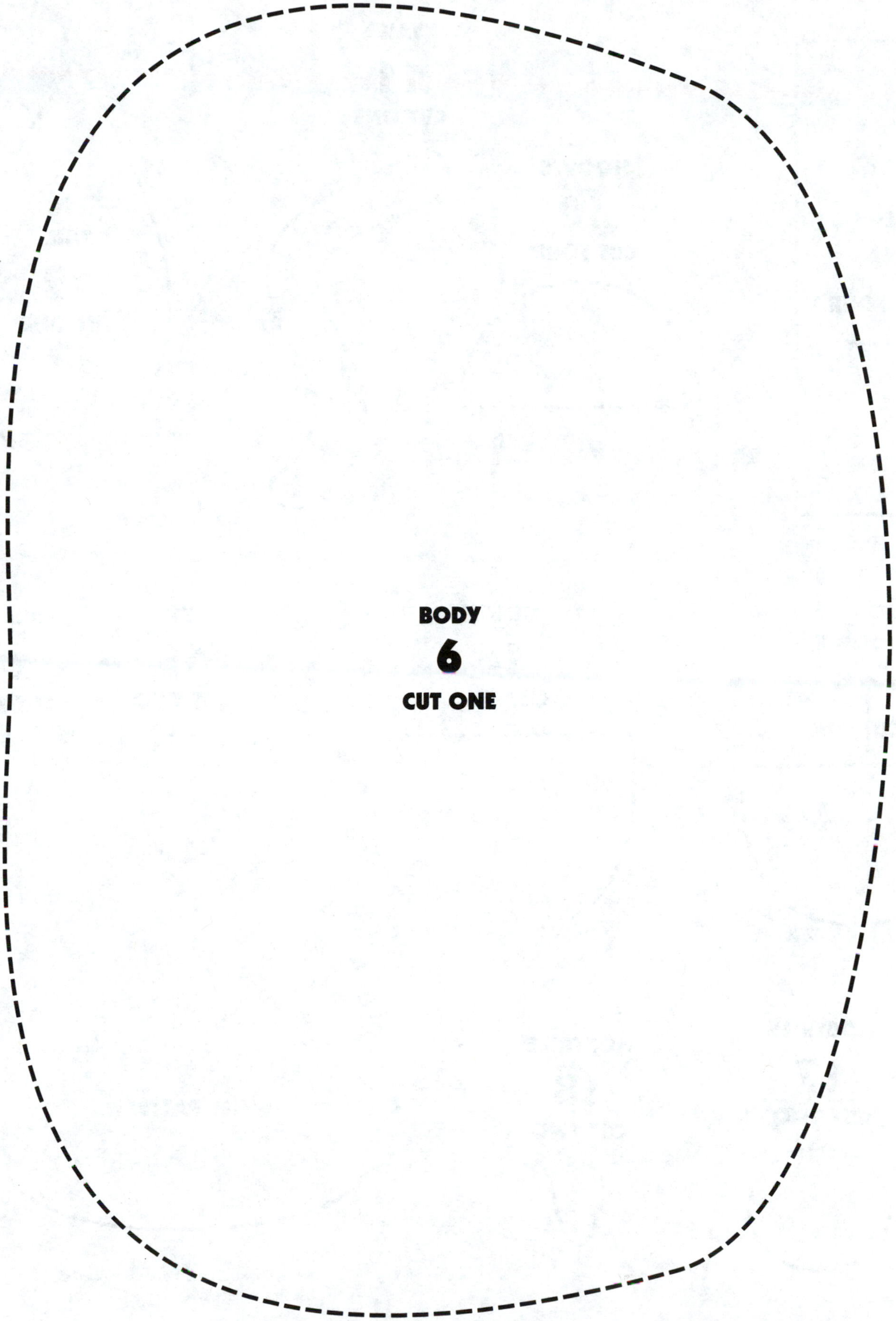

BODY
6
CUT ONE

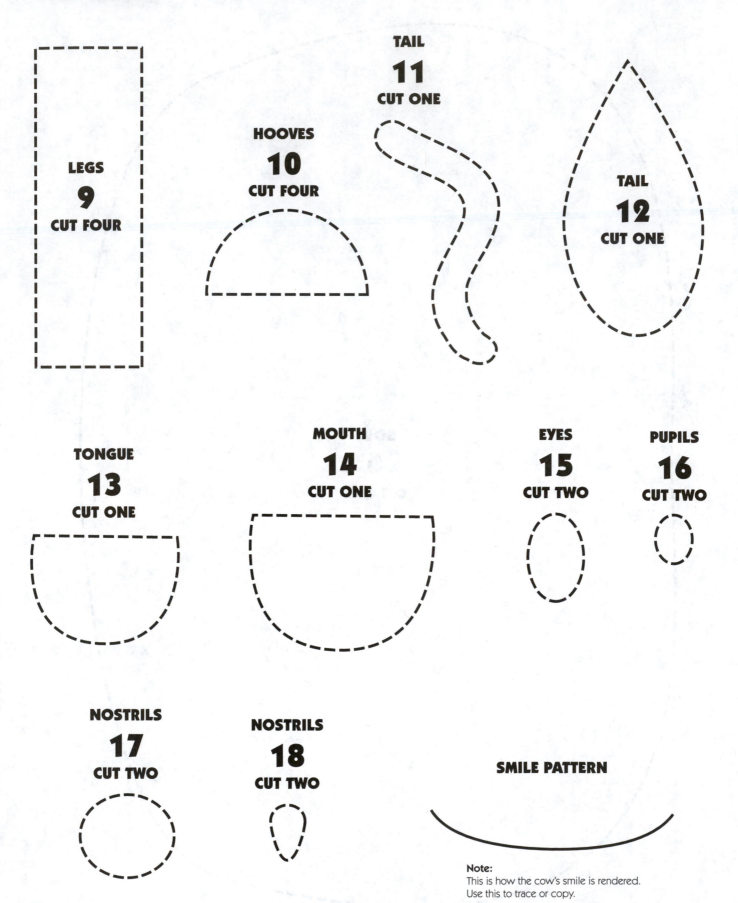

TAIL
11
CUT ONE

HOOVES
10
CUT FOUR

LEGS
9
CUT FOUR

TAIL
12
CUT ONE

TONGUE
13
CUT ONE

MOUTH
14
CUT ONE

EYES
15
CUT TWO

PUPILS
16
CUT TWO

NOSTRILS
17
CUT TWO

NOSTRILS
18
CUT TWO

SMILE PATTERN

Note:
This is how the cow's smile is rendered.
Use this to trace or copy.

Materials: *black, brown and tan paper; scissors; glue; black crayon or marker*

DOG

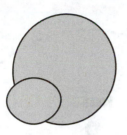

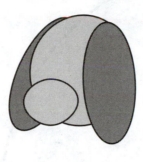

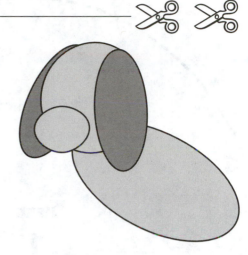

1 Cut one #1 head and one #2 nose from tan paper. Glue the nose on the head as shown.

2 Cut two #3 ears from brown paper and glue one ear to the back of the head and the other ear to the front of the head as shown.

3 Cut one #4 body from tan paper. Glue the headpiece on top of the body as illustrated.

4 Cut one #5 hip from tan paper and glue at the bottom of the body. Cut two #6 front legs from tan paper and glue to the front of the body as shown.

5 Cut four #7 feet from tan paper. Glue two to the bottoms of the front legs and two to the back of the dog as shown. Use a black crayon or marker to draw lines on the feet for toes and to draw on the nose and mouth.

6 Cut one #8 tail from tan paper and glue to the back of the body as shown. Cut two #9 eyes from black paper or use a black marker or crayon the draw on the eyes.

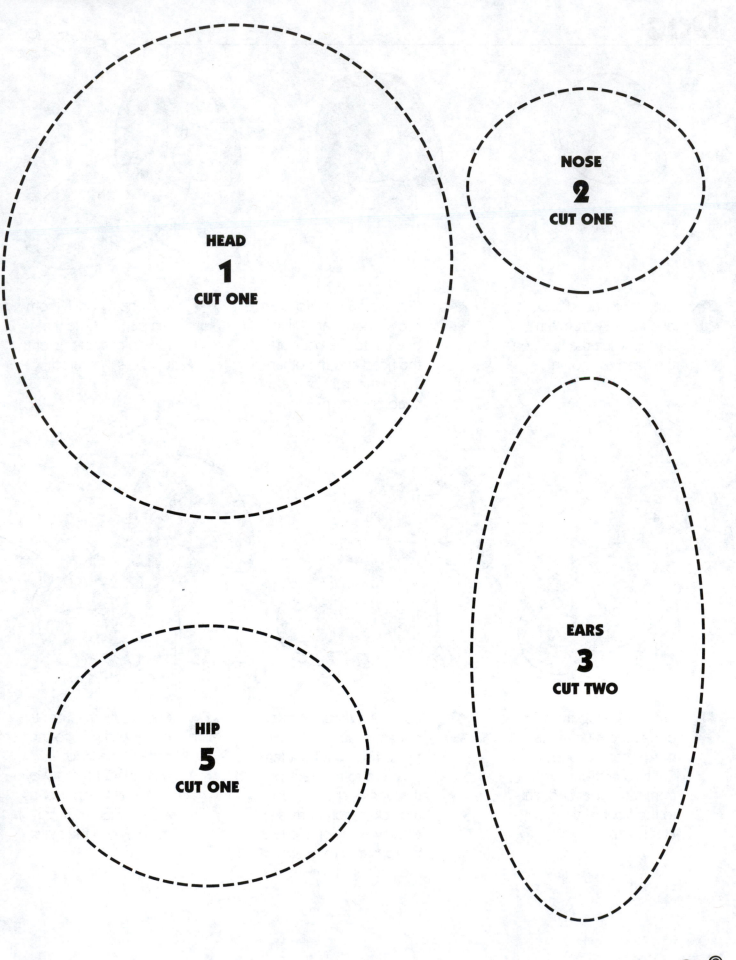

HEAD

1

CUT ONE

NOSE

2

CUT ONE

EARS

3

CUT TWO

HIP

5

CUT ONE

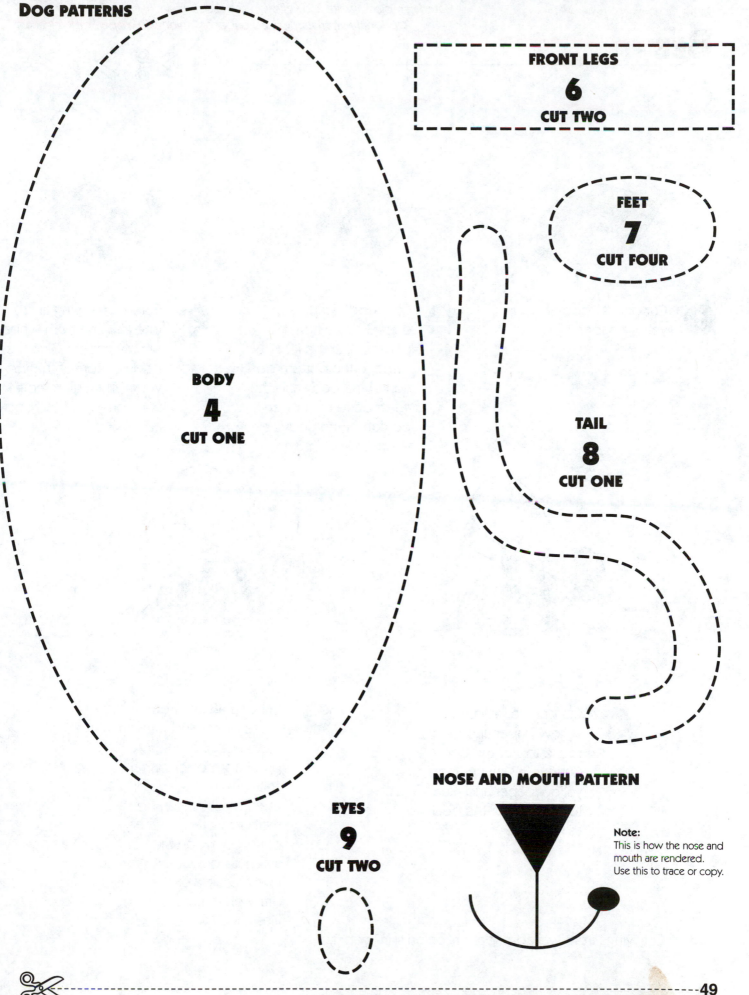

DOG PATTERNS

FRONT LEGS
6
CUT TWO

FEET
7
CUT FOUR

BODY
4
CUT ONE

TAIL
8
CUT ONE

EYES
9
CUT TWO

NOSE AND MOUTH PATTERN

Note:
This is how the nose and mouth are rendered. Use this to trace or copy.

BEE

1 Cut one #1 body from yellow paper.

2 Cut one #2 stripe and one #3 stripe from black paper. Glue the #2 stripe to the bottom portion of the body and the #3 stripe to the upper portion of the body as illustrated.

3 Cut one #4 wing and one #5 wing from white or gray paper. Glue the body on top of the #5 wing. Then glue the #4 wing on top of the body as shown.

4 Cut one #6 head from yellow paper and glue to the top of the body. Cut one #7 stinger from yellow paper and glue to the back of the body as shown.

5 Cut one #8 eye from white paper and glue on the head. Cut one #9 pupil from black paper and glue on the eye or use a black crayon or marker to draw on the pupil. Draw on the antennas or glue on chenille pipe cleaners. Draw on the mouth as illustrated.

Note: Cut wings from waxed paper or "onion skin" paper.

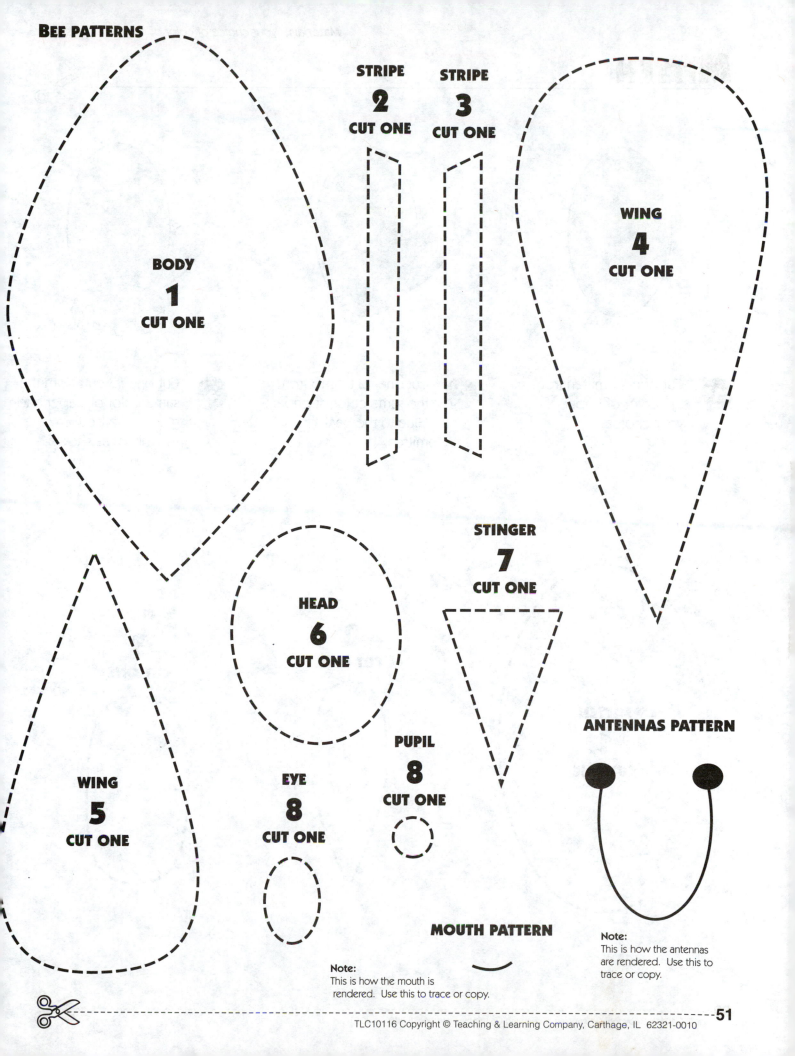

BEE PATTERNS

STRIPE **2** CUT ONE

STRIPE **3** CUT ONE

WING **4** CUT ONE

BODY **1** CUT ONE

STINGER **7** CUT ONE

HEAD **6** CUT ONE

ANTENNAS PATTERN

WING **5** CUT ONE

EYE **8** CUT ONE

PUPIL **8** CUT ONE

MOUTH PATTERN

Note:
This is how the mouth is rendered. Use this to trace or copy.

Note:
This is how the antennas are rendered. Use this to trace or copy.

Materials: *your choice of color of paper, scissors, glue*

MITTEN

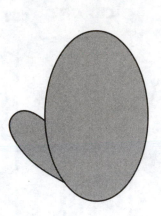

1 Cut one #1 mitten from the color of paper of your choice.

2 Cut one #2 thumb from the same color of paper. Glue to the back of the mitten.

3 Cut one #3 cuff from the same color of paper and glue to the bottom of the mitten as shown.

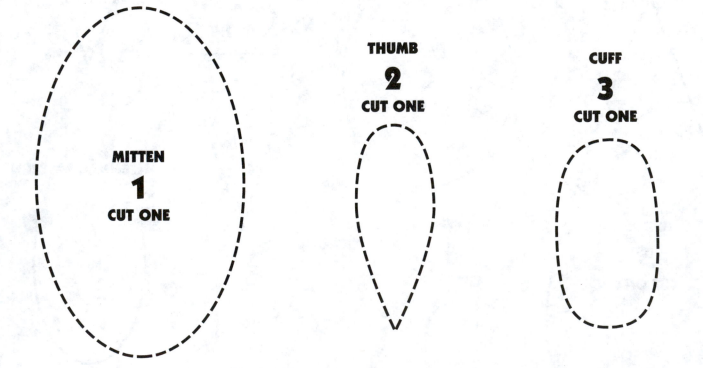

MITTEN

1

CUT ONE

THUMB

2

CUT ONE

CUFF

3

CUT ONE

MOUSE

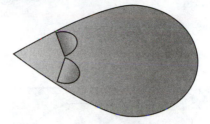 

1 Cut one #1 body from gray paper. Cut two #2 ears from gray paper and glue to the body as shown.

2 Cut two #3 inner ears from pink paper and glue to the tops of the #2 ears. Cut one #4 nose from pink paper and glue to the tip of the body as illustrated.

3 Cut two #5 eyes from white paper and glue to the body. Cut two #6 pupils from black paper and glue on the eyes as shown, or draw on the pupils with a black crayon or marker. Cut one #7 tail from gray paper and glue to the back of the body.

Note: Omit eye pattern pieces and glue on wiggly eyes instead.

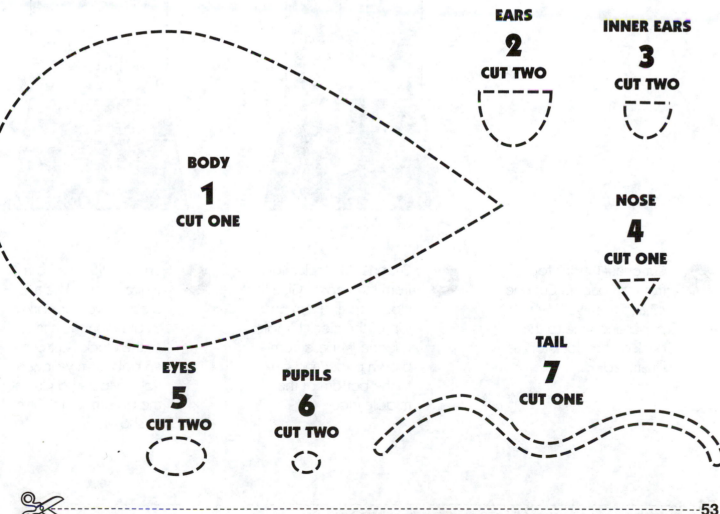

BODY
1
CUT ONE

EARS
2
CUT TWO

INNER EARS
3
CUT TWO

NOSE
4
CUT ONE

EYES
5
CUT TWO

PUPILS
6
CUT TWO

TAIL
7
CUT ONE

Materials: *brown, tan, white and yellow paper; scissors; glue; black crayon or marker*

CLOCK

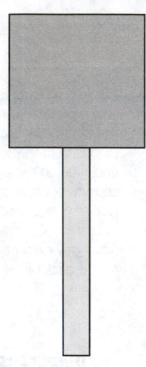

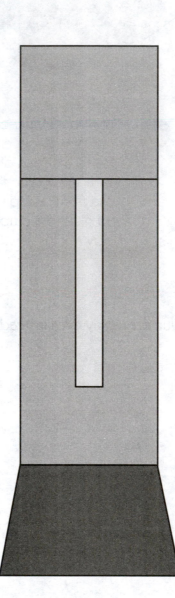

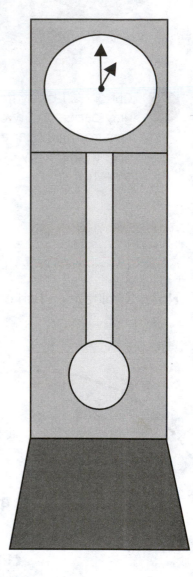

 1 Cut one #1 clock top from tan paper. Cut one #2 arm from yellow paper and glue to the back of the clock top as illustrated.

2 Cut one #3 clock middle from tan paper. Glue the clock top and arm on top of the clock middle. Cut one #4 base from brown paper and glue to the bottom of the middle clock.

3 Cut one #5 face from white paper. Use a black crayon or marker to draw on the hands of the clock. Cut one #6 bob from yellow or gold paper and glue at the bottom of the arm as shown.

CLOCK PATTERNS

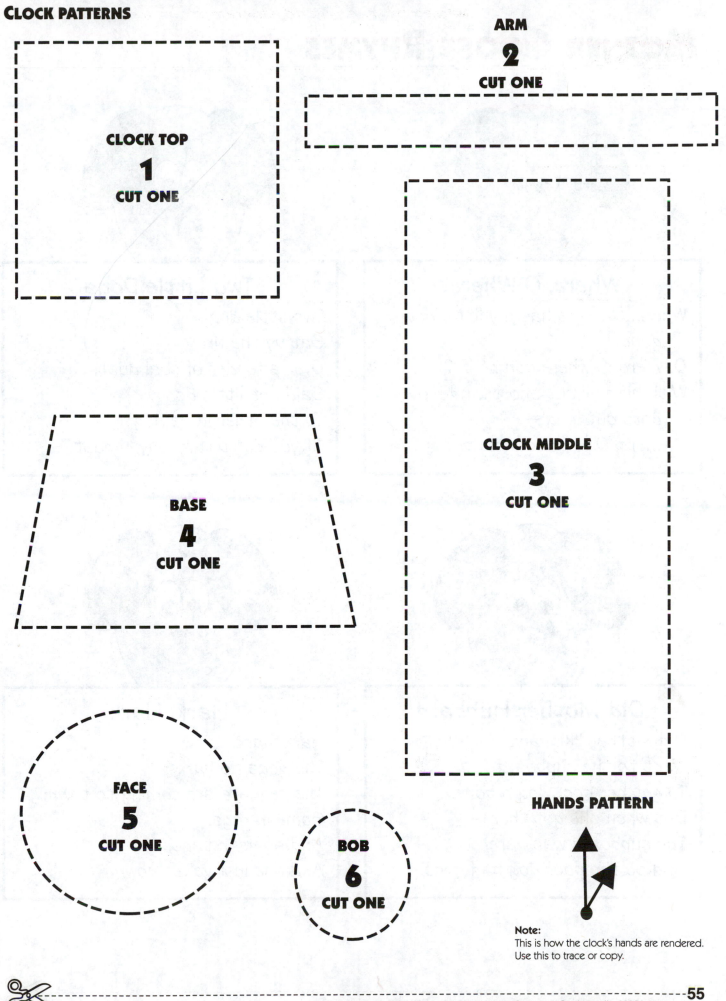

ARM
2
CUT ONE

CLOCK TOP
1
CUT ONE

CLOCK MIDDLE
3
CUT ONE

BASE
4
CUT ONE

FACE
5
CUT ONE

BOB
6
CUT ONE

HANDS PATTERN

Note:
This is how the clock's hands are rendered.
Use this to trace or copy.

MOTHER GOOSE RHYMES

Where, O Where?

Where, O where has my little dog
    gone?
O where, O where can he be?
With his tail cut short, and his
    ears cut long—
O where, O where can he be?

Two Little Dogs

Two little dogs
Sat by the fire,
Over a fender of coal dust;
Said one little dog
To the other little dog,
"If you don't talk, why, I must."

Old Mother Hubbard

Old Mother Hubbard
Went to the cupboard
To get her poor dog a bone.
But when she got there
The cupboard was bare,
And so the poor dog had none.

Hark, Hark

Hark, hark,
The dogs do bark.
The beggars are coming to town;
Some in rags,
And some in tags,
And one in a velvet gown.

DOG

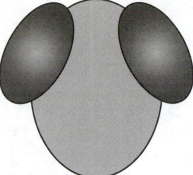

1 Cut one #1 head from tan paper.

2 Cut two #2 ears from brown or black paper. Glue the ears to the top of the head as shown.

3 Use a black marker or crayon to draw on the nose and mouth.

4 Cut two #3 eyes from white paper and glue as shown. Cut two #4 pupils from black paper and glue on the eyes or use a black crayon or marker to draw on the pupils.

5 Cut one #5 bone from white paper and glue at an angle to the bottom of the head. Use a marker to write *bone* on it.

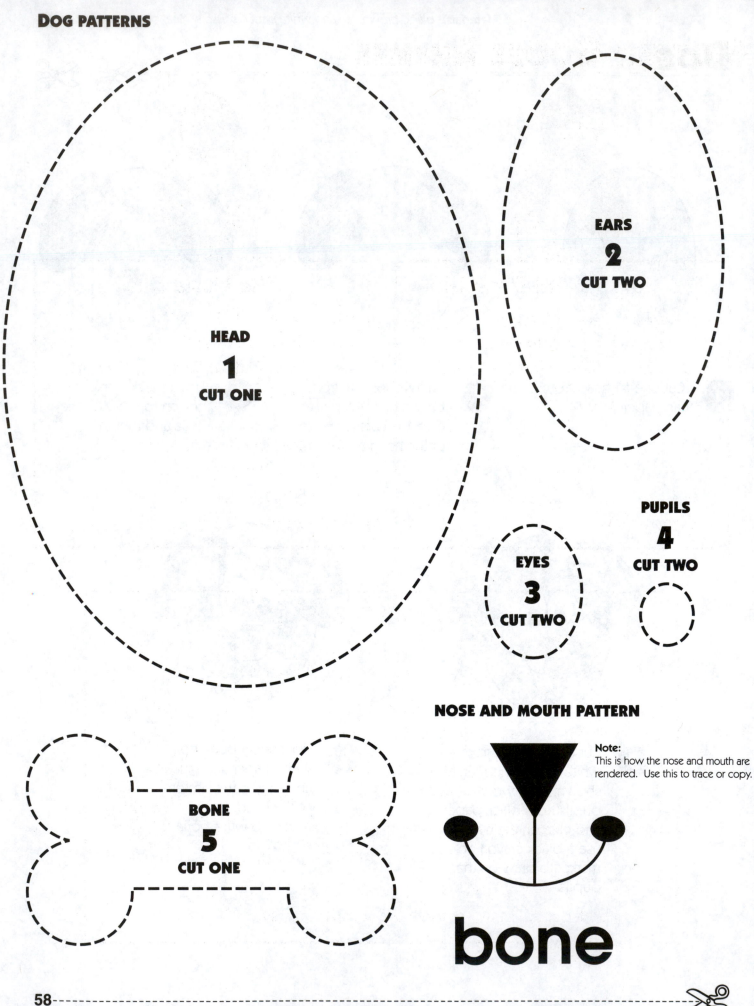

HEAD

1

CUT ONE

EARS

2

CUT TWO

PUPILS

4

CUT TWO

EYES

3

CUT TWO

NOSE AND MOUTH PATTERN

BONE

5

CUT ONE

Note:
This is how the nose and mouth are rendered. Use this to trace or copy.

bone

The North Wind Doth Blow

The north wind doth blow,
And we shall have snow,
And what will the robin do then?
   Poor thing!

He'll sit in the barn
And keep himself warm,
And hide his head under his wing.
   Poor thing!

The Little Bird

Once I saw a little bird
Come hop, hop, hop;
So I cried, "Little bird,
Will you stop, stop, stop?"

And was going to the window
To say, "How do you do?"
But he shook his little tail
And far away he flew.

Little Robin Redbreast

Little Robin Redbreast sat upon a rail;
Niddle-naddle went his head, wiggle-waggle went his tail.

Little Robin Redbreast sat upon a tree,
Up went Pussy Cat, and down went he.

Down came Pussy Cat, and away Robin ran;
Says Little Robin Redbreast, "Catch me if you can."

Little Robin Redbreast jumped upon a wall;
Pussy Cat jumped after him, and almost got a fall.

Little Robin chirped and sang, and what did Pussy say?
Pussy Cat said, "Mew," and Robin jumped away.

Materials: black, brown, orange, pink, tan, white and yellow paper; scissors; glue; black crayon or marker

ROBIN

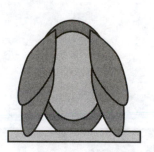

 1 Cut one #1 body from brown paper. Cut one #2 chest from orange paper. Glue the chest on top of the body.

2 Cut one #3 perch from tan paper, and glue to the bottom of the body as illustrated. Cut two #4 wings from brown paper. Glue the wings to the body as shown. Cut two #5 wings from brown paper. Glue these wings on top of the #4 wings as shown.

3 Cut one #6 head from brown paper. Cut two #7 cheeks from pink paper, and glue on the head as shown. Cut two #8 eyes from white paper. Glue the eyes on the head. Cut two #9 pupils from black paper. Glue the pupils on the eyes as shown. Now glue the headpiece on the body.

5 Cut one #10 tail feather and two #11 tail feathers from brown paper. Glue the #11 tail feathers on top of the #10 tail feather. Now glue the feathers to the bottom of the body. Cut six #12 feet from yellow paper. Glue the feet in place as illustrated.

6 Cut one #13 beak and one #14 beak from orange paper. Glue the #13 beak on the head as shown. Now glue the #14 beak on top of the #13 beak as illustrated. With a black crayon or marker, draw on the hair.

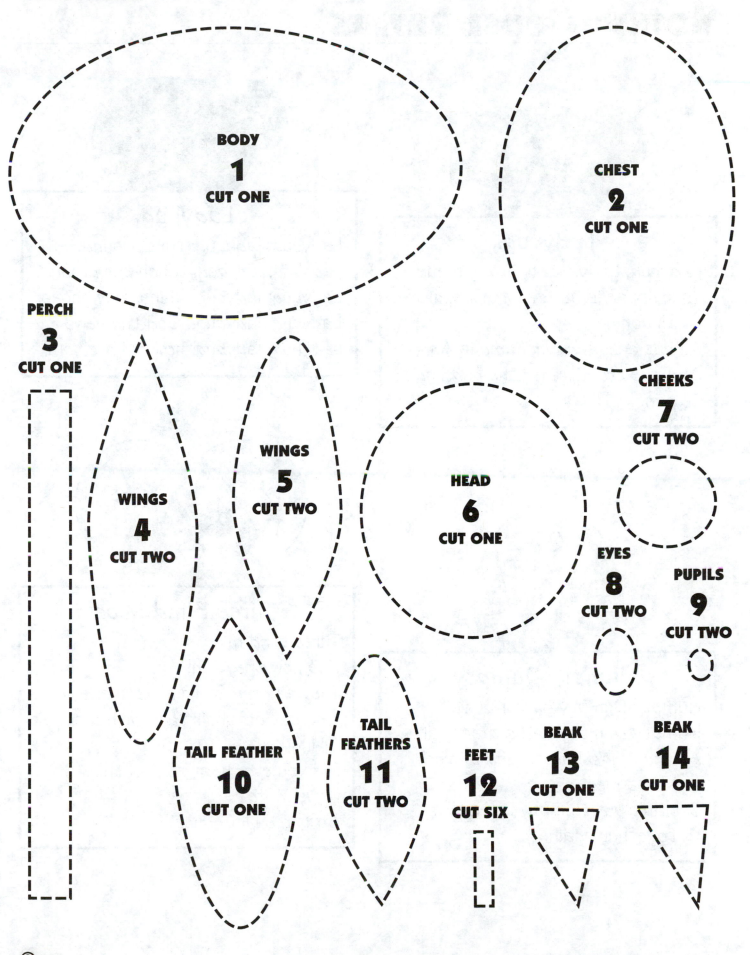

Ladybug!

Ladybug, Ladybug, fly away home.
Your house is on fire, your children
   all gone,
All but one, and her name is Ann,
And she crept under the pudding
   pan.

Ladybug

Ladybug, ladybug, turn around.
Ladybug, ladybug, touch the ground.
Ladybug, ladybug, shine your shoes.
Ladybug, ladybug, read the news.
Ladybug, ladybug, how old are you?

Humpty Dumpty

Humpty Dumpty sat on a wall.
Humpty Dumpty had a great fall.
All the King's horses and all the
   King's men
Couldn't put Humpty Dumpty
   together again.

Three Blind Mice

Three blind mice,
See how they run!
They all ran after the farmer's wife,
Who cut off their tails with a carv-
   ing knife;
Did you ever hear such a thing in
   your life
As three blind mice?

Materials: *black and red paper, scissors, glue, black crayon or marker*
Optional Materials: *brad fasteners*

LADYBUG

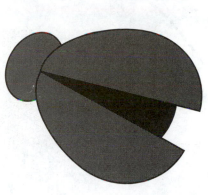

 1 Cut one #1 body from black paper.

2 Cut one #2 head from red paper. Glue the body on the head as shown.

3 Cut two #3 wings from red paper and glue on the body as shown.

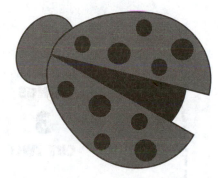

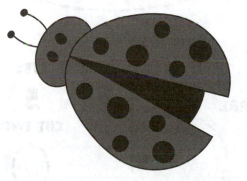

4 Cut several #4 spots from black paper and glue on the wings. You may also use a black marker or crayon to draw on the spots.

5 Cut two #5 eyes from black paper and glue on head or use a black crayon or marker to draw on the eyes. Draw on the antennas or glue on chenille pipe cleaners.

Note: Attach wings at the top with brad fasteners. Write a numeral on the body, then draw that number of spots on the wings.

LADYBUG PATTERNS

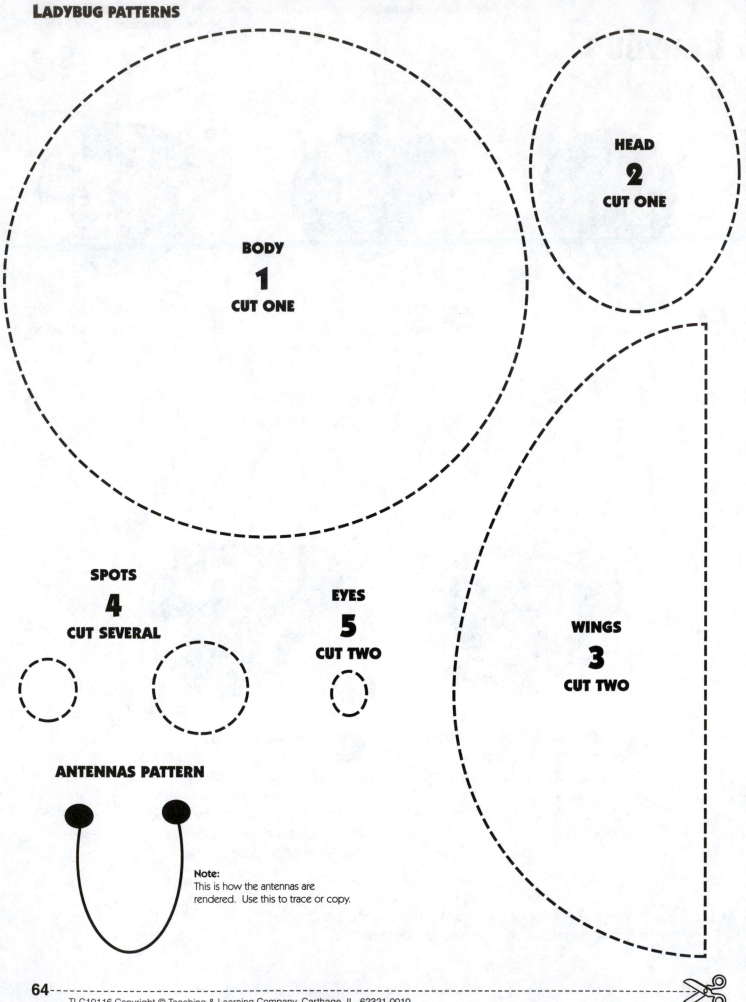

HEAD
2
CUT ONE

BODY
1
CUT ONE

SPOTS
4
CUT SEVERAL

EYES
5
CUT TWO

WINGS
3
CUT TWO

ANTENNAS PATTERN

Note:
This is how the antennas are
rendered. Use this to trace or copy.

Materials: *black, blue, red, white and yellow paper; scissors; glue; black crayon or marker*

HUMPTY DUMPTY

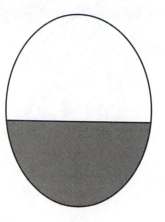

1 Cut one #1 body from white paper. Cut one #2 pants from blue paper. Glue the pants to the bottom of the body.

2 Cut two #3 arms from red paper and glue as shown.

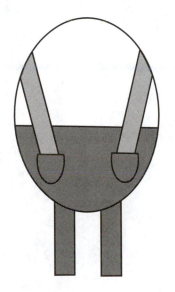

3 Cut two #4 pockets from blue paper and glue over the ends of the arms as shown. Cut two #5 legs from blue paper and glue to the back of the body as illustrated.

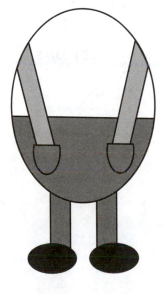

4 Cut two #6 feet from black paper and glue on the bottoms of the legs.

5 Cut two #7 eyes from yellow paper. Draw the pupils on the eyes with a black crayon or marker. Also draw on the mouth as illustrated. Cut three #8 buttons from black paper and glue on the pants.

BODY

1

CUT ONE

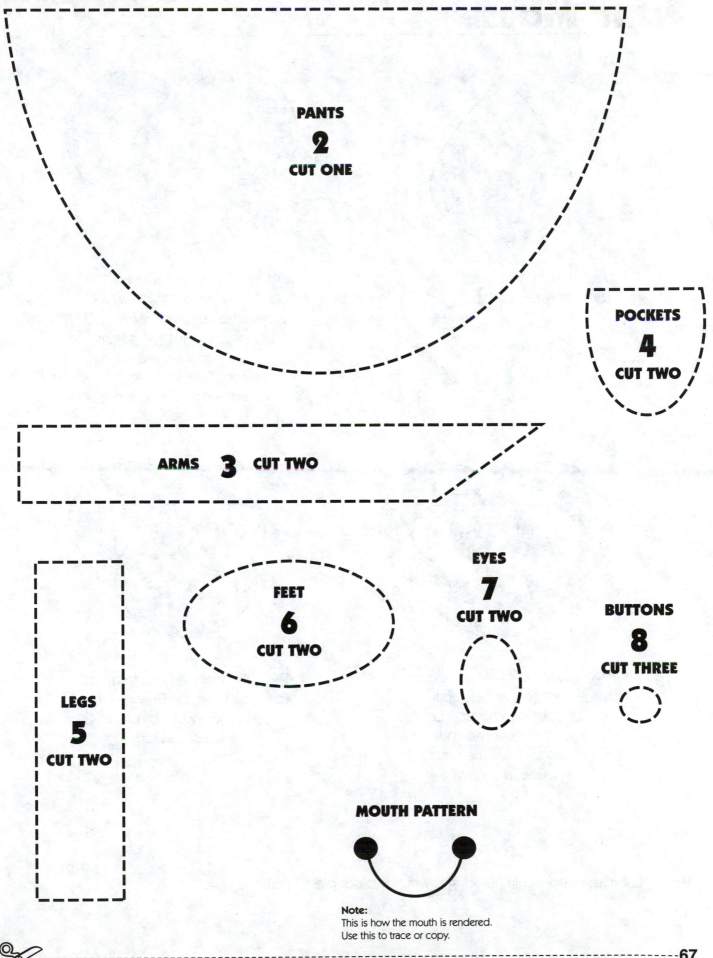

PANTS
2
CUT ONE

POCKETS
4
CUT TWO

ARMS **3** CUT TWO

EYES
7
CUT TWO

BUTTONS
8
CUT THREE

FEET
6
CUT TWO

LEGS
5
CUT TWO

MOUTH PATTERN

Note:
This is how the mouth is rendered.
Use this to trace or copy.

Materials: black, dark gray, gray and pink paper; scissors; glue; black crayon or marker
Optional Materials: black gift wrap paper or black plastic garbage bags

BLIND MOUSE

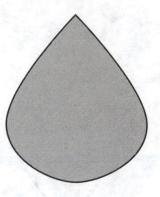

1 Cut one #1 head from gray paper.

2 Cut two #2 ears from gray paper. Cut two #3 inner ears from pink paper. Glue the #3 ears on the #2 ears as shown. Then glue each set of ears to the back of the head as shown.

3 Cut two #4 glasses from dark gray or black paper. Cut one #5 nosepiece from dark gray or black paper. Glue the pieces in place as shown.

4 Cut one #6 nose from pink paper. Draw on the mouth with a black crayon or marker.

Note: Cut glasses from shiny black gift wrap or black plastic garbage bags.

BLIND MOUSE PATTERNS

INNER EARS

3

CUT TWO

HEAD

1

CUT ONE

GLASSES

4

CUT TWO

NOSEPIECE

5

CUT ONE

NOSE

6

CUT ONE

EARS

2

CUT TWO

MOUTH PATTERN

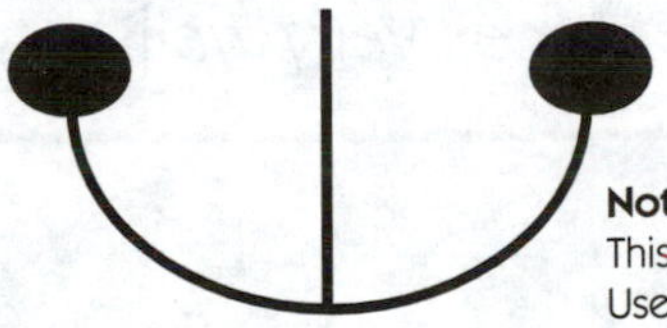

Note:
This is how the mouth is rendered.
Use this to trace or copy.

Rub a Dub, Dub

Rub a dub, dub,
Three men in a tub;
And who do you think they be?
The butcher, the baker,
The candlestick maker;
Toss them out—all three!

Five Monkeys

Five little monkeys jumping on the
    bed.
One fell out and hurt his head.
The rest called the doctor,
And the doctor said,
"That is what you get for jumping
    on the bed."

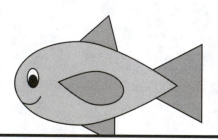

I Caught a Fish

1, 2, 3, 4, 5!
Once I caught a fish alive;
6, 7, 8, 9, 10!
I let him go again.

Peter, Peter, Pumpkin Eater

Peter, Peter, pumpkin eater,
Had a wife and couldn't keep her.
He put her in a pumpkin shell,
And there he kept her very well.

Materials: *black, blue, brown, flesh-colored, red, tan and white paper; scissors; glue; black crayon or marker*
Optional Materials: *corrugated cardboard*

THREE MEN IN A TUB

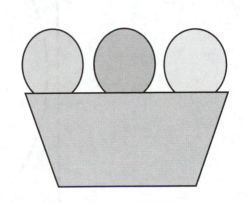

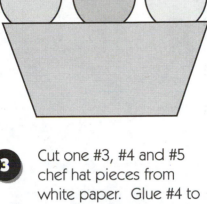

1 Cut one #1 tub from tan paper.

2 Cut three #2 heads from different flesh-colored paper. Glue in place as shown.

3 Cut one #3, #4 and #5 chef hat pieces from white paper. Glue #4 to the back of #3 and #5 at the bottom of #4 as shown. Cut three #6 hair pieces from brown paper and glue to top of the third head.

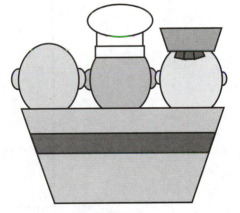

4 Cut six #7 ears from the same color of paper you used for each head and glue on the appropriate heads. Cut one #8 hat from blue paper for the candlestick maker.

5 Cut one #9 stripe from red paper and glue on the tub as shown.

6 Use the facial features patterns provided on page 74 or use a black marker or crayon to draw on the faces of your men.

Note: Cut tub from thin corrugated cardboard.

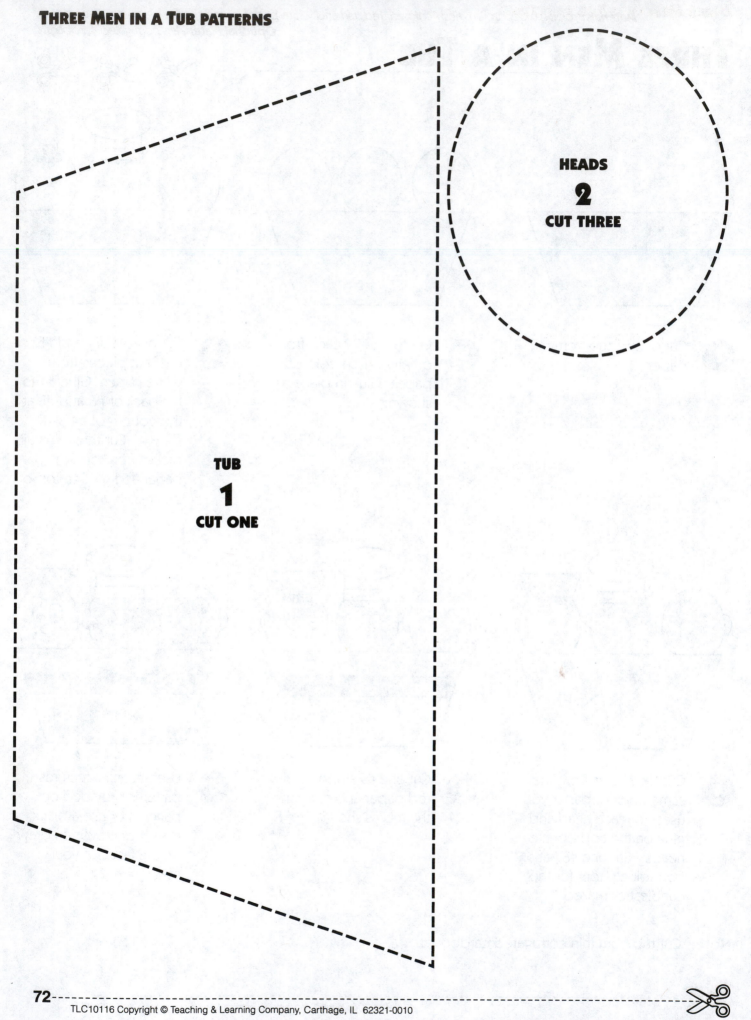

HEADS

2

CUT THREE

TUB

1

CUT ONE

Three Men in a Tub Patterns

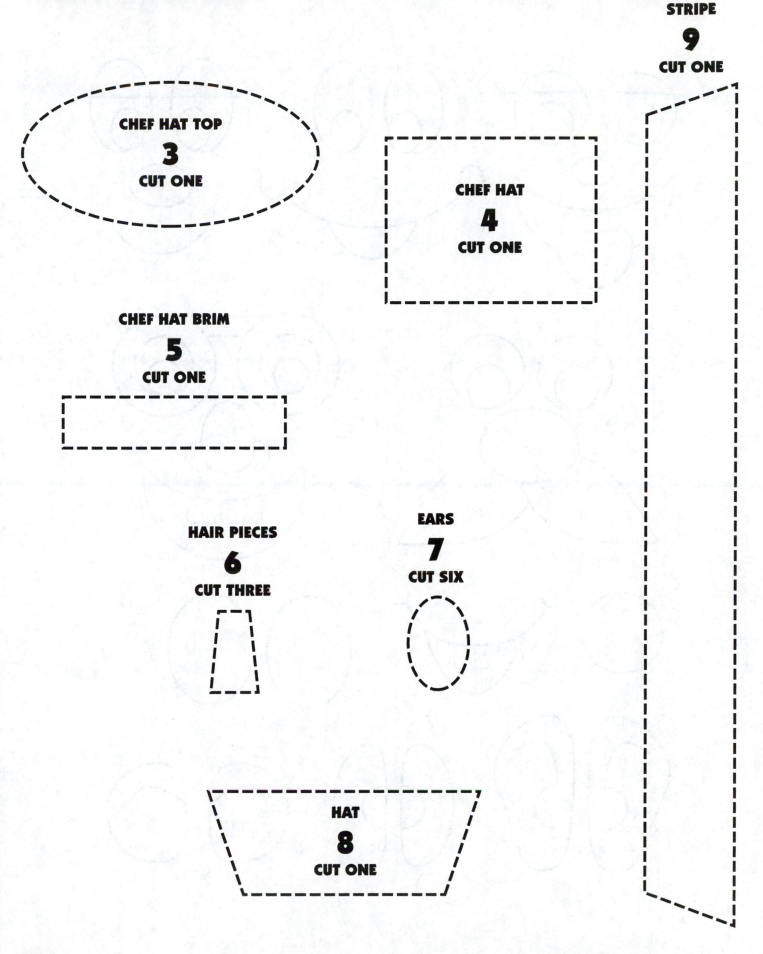

STRIPE

9

CUT ONE

CHEF HAT TOP

3

CUT ONE

CHEF HAT

4

CUT ONE

CHEF HAT BRIM

5

CUT ONE

HAIR PIECES

6

CUT THREE

EARS

7

CUT SIX

HAT

8

CUT ONE

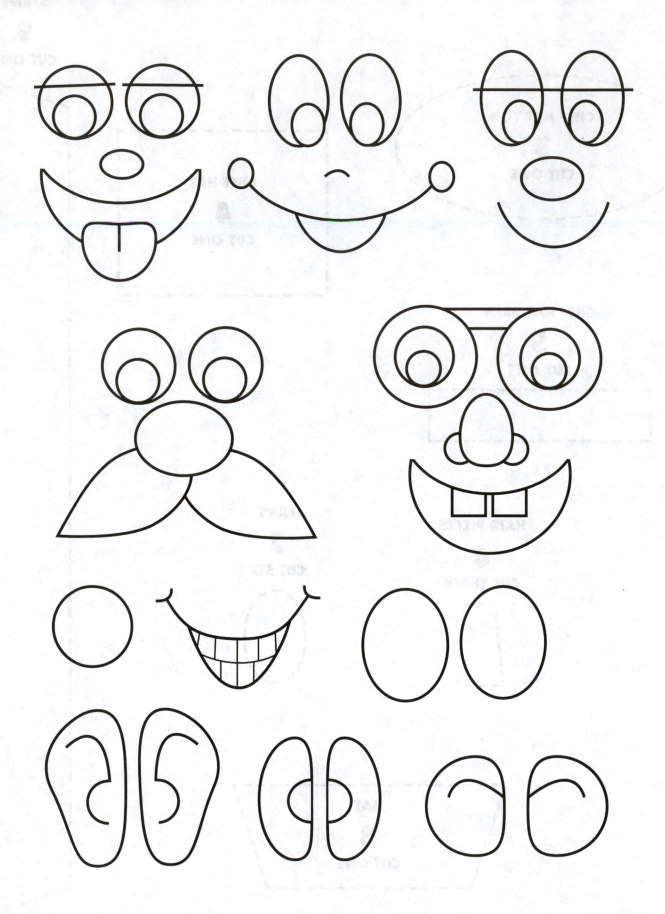

Materials: black, dark green, light green and white paper; scissors; glue; black crayon or marker
Optional Materials: metallic gift wrap or wallpaper samples

FISH

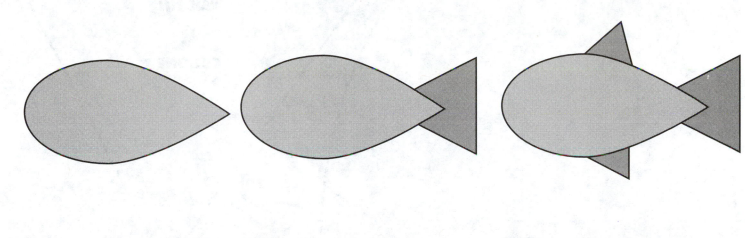

1 Cut one #1 body from light green paper.

2 Cut one #2 tail fin from dark green paper and glue to the back of the body as shown.

3 Cut two #3 fins from dark green paper and glue one to back of the top of the body and one to the bottom of the body as shown.

4 Cut one #4 fin from dark green paper and glue in the middle of the body.

5 Cut one #5 eye from white paper and glue in place as shown. Cut one #6 pupil from black paper and glue on the eye. Use a black crayon or marker to draw on the mouth.

Note: Cut fish pieces from pieces of metallic gift wrap or wallpaper samples.

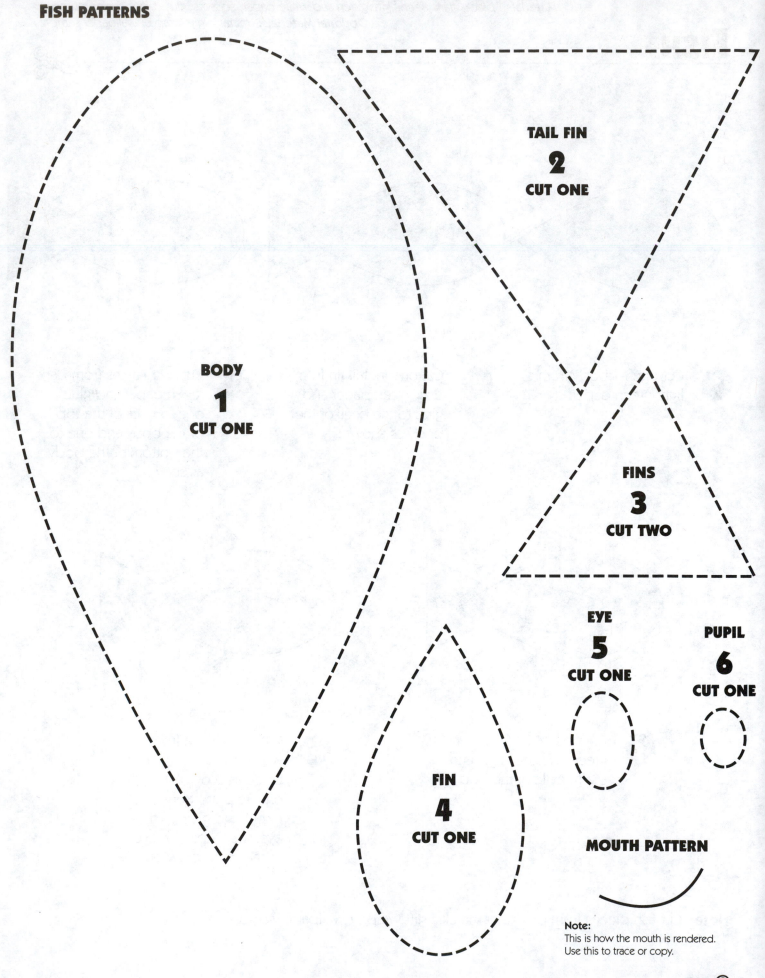

TAIL FIN
2
CUT ONE

BODY
1
CUT ONE

FINS
3
CUT TWO

EYE
5
CUT ONE

PUPIL
6
CUT ONE

FIN
4
CUT ONE

MOUTH PATTERN

Note:
This is how the mouth is rendered.
Use this to trace or copy.

MONKEY

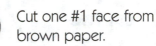

1 Cut one #1 face from brown paper.

2 Cut one #2 head from brown paper. Glue the face on top of the head as shown.

3 Cut two #3 ears from brown paper. Cut two #4 inner ears from tan paper. Glue the #4 ears on top of the #3 ears; then glue each set of ears to the back of the head and face as shown.

4 Cut one #5 tongue from red paper and glue in place. Use a black crayon or marker to draw on the mouth.

5 Cut two #6 nostrils from black paper and glue on the face as shown. Cut two #7 eyes from black paper and glue on the head as shown.

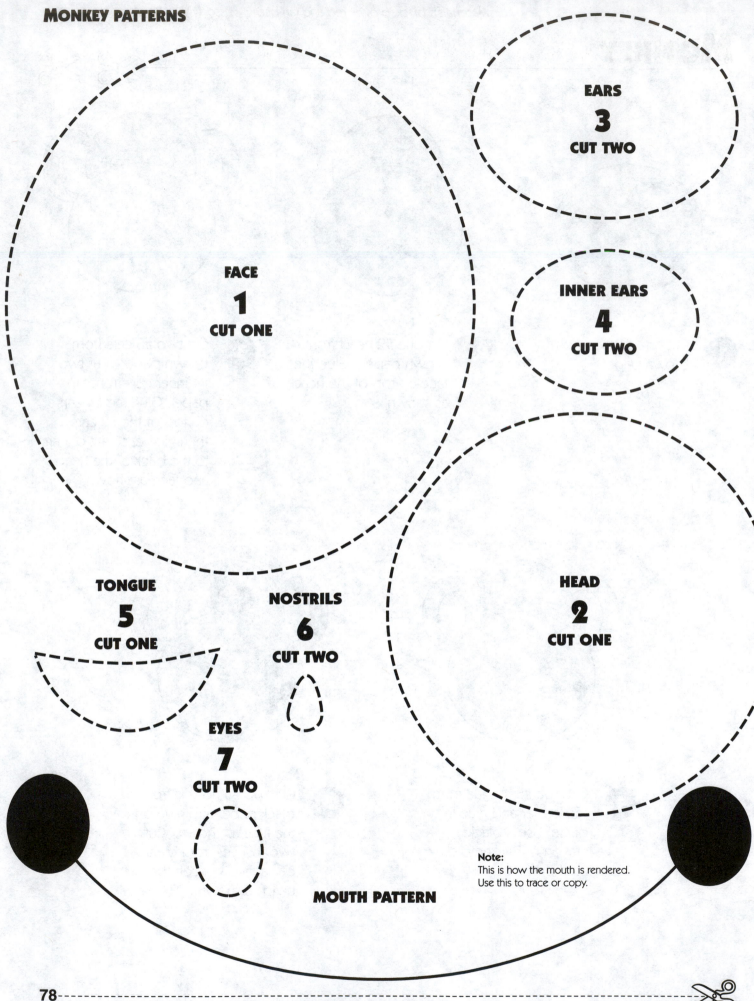

FACE
1
CUT ONE

EARS
3
CUT TWO

INNER EARS
4
CUT TWO

HEAD
2
CUT ONE

TONGUE
5
CUT ONE

NOSTRILS
6
CUT TWO

EYES
7
CUT TWO

Note:
This is how the mouth is rendered.
Use this to trace or copy.

MOUTH PATTERN

Materials: black, brown, flesh-colored, green, orange, red, white and yellow paper; scissors; glue; black crayon or marker

Optional Materials: paper plates

PETER, PETER, PUMPKIN EATER

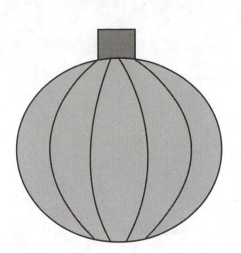

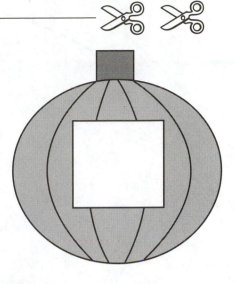

1 Cut one #1 pumpkin from orange paper.

2 Cut one #2 stem from brown or green paper and glue to the back of the pumpkin at the top. With a black crayon or marker, draw lines on the pumpkin as shown.

3 Cut one #3 window from white paper. Glue in the center of the pumpkin.

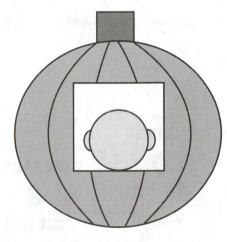

4 Cut one #4 head and two #5 ears from flesh-colored paper. Glue the ears to the back of the head and then paste in the window.

5 Cut two #6 hair pieces from brown paper and glue to the top of the head. Cut two #7 bows and one #8 bow center from red paper. Glue the two points of the #7 bows together; then glue the #8 bow center on top as shown. Paste the completed bow to the head as illustrated.

6 Use the facial features patterns on page 74 or use a black marker or crayon to draw the face on your woman.

Note: Use a small, orange paper plate for the pumpkin shape.

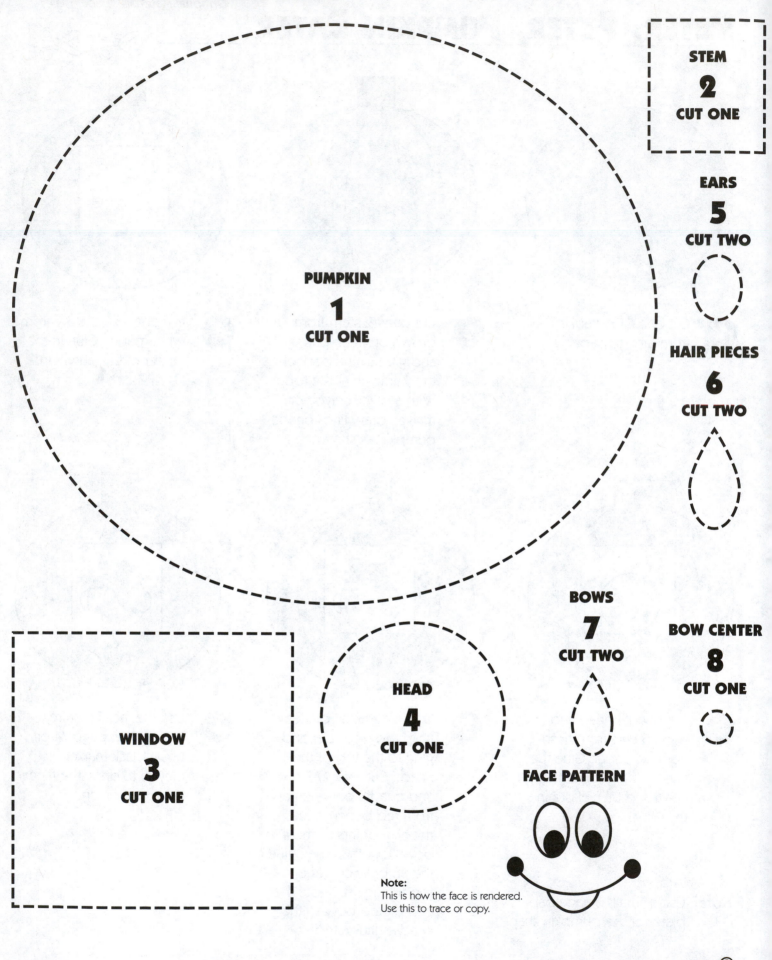

STEM

2

CUT ONE

EARS

5

CUT TWO

HAIR PIECES

6

CUT TWO

PUMPKIN

1

CUT ONE

BOWS

7

CUT TWO

BOW CENTER

8

CUT ONE

HEAD

4

CUT ONE

WINDOW

3

CUT ONE

FACE PATTERN

Note:
This is how the face is rendered.
Use this to trace or copy.